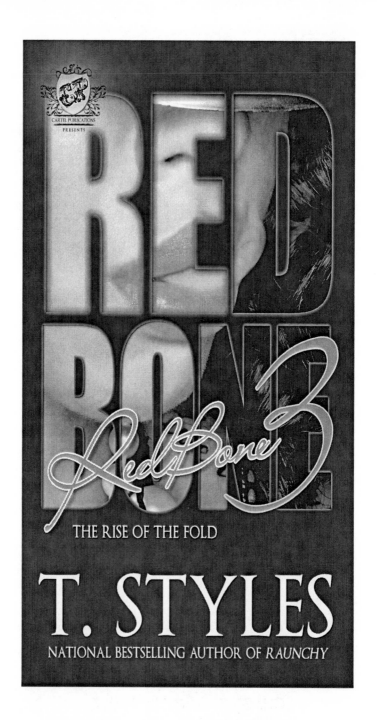

RED BONE 3

RedBone

THE RISE OF THE FOLD

T. STYLES

NATIONAL BESTSELLING AUTHOR OF *RAUNCHY*

CHECK OUT OTHER TITLES BY THE CARTEL PUBLICATIONS

REDBONE 3: THE RISE OF THE FOLD

WWW.THECARTELPUBLICATIONS.COM

By T. STYLES

PUBLISHER'S NOTE:
This book is a work of fiction. Names,
characters, businesses,
Organizations, places, events and incidents
are the product of the
Author's imagination or are used fictionally.
Any resemblance of
Actual persons, living or dead, events, or
locales are entirely coincidental.

Library of Congress Control Number: 2016934345

ISBN 10: 0996209921

ISBN 13: 978-0996209922

Cover Design: Davida Baldwin
www.oddballdsgn.com

www.thecartelpublications.com

First Edition

Printed in the United States of America

By T. STYLES   7

REDBONE 3:

"The Rise Of The Fold"

By T. Styles

What's Up Fam,

I normally don't do this, but I feel I must. This is an election year and I need all of you reading this book, that are of voting age, to make your vote count. We can't complain about the issues of today if we don't do our part by trying to place the most qualified and logical people in place to run our government.

Aight, now that the PSA is out of the way ☺ I'ma jump right in because I can't wait any longer!

In preparation for this book dropping I read, "Redbone 2" again to give myself a refresher. Lawd Have Mercy... T. Styles went above and beyond on this one! "Redbone 3: The Rise of The Fold" is a MASTERFUL work of literary art. I was pulled into this story from the first page. I KNOW you are going to go through an assortment of emotions reading this novel.

Get Ready!!

With that being said, keeping in line with tradition, we want to give respect to a vet or trailblazer paving the way. In this novel, we would like to recognize:

Leonardo DiCaprio

Leonardo Wilhelm DiCaprio is the phenomenal American actor and Environmental Philanthropist who has a vast number of accreditations and roles he has attained and performed. Some of my favorite movies from him are, *The Man in The Iron Mask*; *What's Eating Gilbert Grape?*; *Catch me If You Can*; *The Departed*; *The Wolf of Wall Street*; *DJango* and of course his most recent movie, *The Revenant.*

He FINALLY won the Academy Award this year (2016) for his role and outstanding performance in The Revenant, which was well deserved and way overdue. If you have not seen any of his films, please do yourself a favor and get aquatinted, you will be glad you did.

Aight, get to it. I'll catch you in the next novel.

Be Easy!

Charisse "C. Wash" Washington
Vice President
The Cartel Publications
www.thecartelpublications.com
www.facebook.com/publishercwash
Instagram: publishercwash
www.twitter.com/cartelbooks
www.facebook.com/cartelpublications
Follow us on Instagram: Cartelpublications
#CartelPublications
#UrbanFiction
#LeonardoDiCaprio
#PrayForCeCe

CARTEL URBAN CINEMA'S 1st MOVIE

PITBULLS IN A SKIRT – THE MOVIE

NOW AVAILABLE:

DVD/AMAZON STREAMING

www.cartelurbancinema.com and

www.amazon.com

www.thecartelpublications.com

By T. STYLES   11

#Redbone3

PROLOGUE

CUTIE TUDY'S HOUSE

Washington, DC

PRESENT DAY

It was tough watching a whore in action and yet Cutie Tudy was forced to do just that...

Body damp from the night's rain that continued to drown out the city, the large brown sofa swallowed Cutie as she eyed her trashy foster mother Melinda Sheldon across the way. The decent thing would've been to carry the spectacle to her room but neither Melinda nor Jones, the driver who she failed to pay due to brokeness, had the time or the inclination.

When he learned she was destitute he started to do the American thing and call the cops. Luckily for her he held out and was rewarded by Melinda's snatch swallowing his stiffness on the living room couch.

And to think, all of this jumped off directly after Mooney's funeral earlier that day and Cutie was still morose after losing such a superior friend. But no one gave a fuck, at least not in her apartment anyway. This emotion was causing her to fall deeper into despair.

As she gaped at the show she still couldn't believe a kid she knew murdered her friend. The same person she let finger pump her in the laundry room. A boy she thought liked her— at least a little.

She was wrong.

The day Mooney was murdered started simple enough. Cutie was arm in arm with No Good Naylor from up the block. Although he was easy on the eyes, he was a seventeen-year-old know-it-all who was leading Cutie into a dark laundry room, where his friends were hidden to record video. After a few indiscretions in the under lit space, Mooney snaked into the basement and blew up the teenagers' spot by gunpoint, angering Naylor to no end. He promised to avenge his embarrassment and as a display of his gratitude, later that night he murdered the woman, leaving Cutie virtually alone.

Cutie blinked a few times and noticed Melinda's white bra strap dangling off the side of her body as Jones' fingertips dug into the flesh of her waist, leaving huge dips into her skin. He pumped so hard into her pussy that one of her breast flew out of her slinky grey shirt and slapped against his dry, cracked mouth. Like a tennis racquet he caught her nipple against his lip and sucked for dear life.

They were doing *The Most* in front of the junior as they operated carefree.

When the driver's gaze fell on Cutie Tudy he looked at her lustfully and winked. He was an amateur. Most of Melinda's men flashed a shot of dick to get a rise out of her. It wasn't the first time one of her foster mother's visitants noticed her and with her prostitute type ways, she was certain it wouldn't be the last. At the end of the day Melinda used sex in lieu of money so strangers were normality in the apartment.

Having seen enough Cutie peeled herself off the sofa and stomped toward her room, slamming the door. Flopping on the edge of the bed she observed her face in the large dresser mirror across the way. Her long black hair was plastered to her warm ivory colored skin that was splotched with what looked like smeared red kisses.

Why did losing Mooney hurt so?

She had no idea she would miss the old bird so much, the only bright side being that Naylor and his accomplice was arrested for her slaying directly afterwards.

But when would the pain decease?

Uncomfortable, Cutie removed her wet clothing, plummeted to her knees and hauled the box from under the bed that she'd stolen from Mooney's apartment. Inside was a plethora of information on Farah Cotton and

The Fold, which had recently become her obsession.

Removing a black leather book with raised red letters from the pile, she stumbled over to the light and turned it off before convening on the bed and caressing the thick cool texture. On her mattress she turned on the lamp and eased deeper into the thickness of her bubble gum colored comforter. With her back against the head post she hulled back the cover of the book.

A grin spread across her face as she viewed what she believed was Farah's handwriting.

"Okay, Farah Cotton...tell me the rest of your story," she whispered. "Please."

CHAPTER ONE

FARAH COTTON

"Let's Not Forget About The Hunt."

On top of Bones' black and red handcrafted wooden bed, elevated from the floor just so, Farah gazed down at him as she rocked her hips smoothly, his thickness tucked inside the walls of her pussy like a gun inside a holster. Her sandy brown bob swept against the sides of her angular face as she moaned.

Whenever Bones looked upon her his stare was intense. As if having her in his presence, amongst The Fold, would end at anytime. His obsession growing daily, his greatest fear was that she would withdraw from his life, something he would never tolerate due to his possessiveness.

When Farah felt him pulsating she leaned

to her left where Zashay sat patiently on her knees waiting to serve the couple. Cascades of her fire truck colored hair poured down her brown shoulders making her even more alluring.

Using the golden razor blade that sat in the cup of her red bra, Farah removed it and sliced into the flesh of Zashay's upper arm, just how Farah liked it. Overcome with lust Farah snaked her shiny pink tongue along the red trail oozing from her flesh and sucked lightly, causing Zashay to whimper.

More aroused, Farah's pussy juice drizzled along the shaft of Bones' dick turning his chocolate stick icy white. She felt her euphoria coming on in any minute.

As if she were heavier than 20 kilos of cocaine, Farah's body slammed into Bones' muscular chest, her breast pushing against his toasty body.

Wanting to feel her skin he removed her bra, flinging it on the floor.

On all fours Zashay eased between them, and positioned her body so she could run her tongue along the outer walls of Bones' dick as it slipped in and out of Farah's creamy pussy.

With Zashay turning the fuck fest up a notch, Bones gripped at Farah's breast and sucked her nipple causing Farah to erupt. Always the attentive type, Bones gave her other breast the same treatment even though she was already satisfied. He was willing to continue to suck until Zashay's tongue slid into the cheeks of his asshole, causing him to explode into Farah's flesh.

"Damn, Farah, you...you got me going, baby," he said giving her all the credit and Zashay none of the glory.

"That's one thing we do greatly together," she moaned. "If nothing else."

He wiped her natural hair behind her ear and looked down into her yellow face. "Love me, Farah. I need you to love me."

Zashay cleared her throat. "Excuse me?"

Both Farah and Bones laughed. "Sorry, sexy," Bones said winking at her. "Forgot you were down there."

"I can see that. So I guess ya'll got yours again and leaving me hanging," Zashay pouted, hoping the threesome's adventure would last well into the night. "Besides I was just getting started."

Bones looked down at Farah who's eyes appeared heavy and said, "I'm sorry, Z, but I don't think we got a minute more in us."

"You know what,"— she slid off the bed, snatched her red and black robe marked with 'THE FOLD' logo on the chest and slipped it on— "Don't call me when ya'll need help in the future." She switched out the door, leaving it open.

Farah sighed. "Why's she getting so serious all of a sudden?" She grabbed one of his neat dreads that hung along the sides of his shoulders and wrapped it around her index finger. He kept his hair fresh which was one of the things she appreciated about him. "She knows what it is when we get together."

Bones sighed. "It's different with Zashay." He shrugged. "Members of The Fold feel they should be treated differently if INVITED while GIVERS don't."

"We can't vet Givers right now, Bones." She sat up and crawled toward the headboard, her back resting against it. "Why not go out and Shikar (Hunt) instead of bringing them here? These days we have to be careful."

He chuckled. "You sure the real reason you don't want Givers is due to jealousy?" He paused "Because if you don't want me to be with an Outsider it's not a problem."

Farah laughed and rolled her eyes. "When have you known me to be jealous, Bones? Name one time I didn't allow you your Taste? Giver or not. I mean didn't we just fuck a bitch together?"

"Then why so heavy?"

"I expressed myself and you aren't hearing me. It's not smart to bring new people here right now, Bones. It's not—"

"You don't think I can protect you?" He asked severing her sentence.

She gazed at him. "They are still searching for me. You know that. Do you actually think they're going to forgive the fact that I killed their brother? Whether in self defense or not?" She moved closer. "You have to be careful on who you allow here even if they're properly vetted. But out there...." Her eyes lit up and seemed to sparkle. "Out there we can do whatever we desire and have the cover of night. I mean don't you miss it? Travelling together and looking for the perfect Givers?"

"You did things differently than we did, Farah. We have a system that has protected us for years. From diseases and everything." He shook his head. "Why do you feel the need to tell me how to run things? Next to Dr. Weil I'm in charge." He pointed at the door.

"Yes, I miss Shikar but it has to be done properly," he continued as he ran his hand alongside her face and exhaled. "Listen, it's been eight months, Farah. They aren't going to look for you, Mia and Shadow forever. In the meantime I feel more comfortable bringing Givers here."

She sighed. "It may have been almost a year but to the Bakers it's like yesterday. Allowing anyone to come into the mansion is opening ourselves up for a trap."

"You're being unreasonable."

Farah sighed and scooted off the bed, snatching her silk red THE FOLD robe off the back of her chair. Bones followed and walked up behind her as she stood in front of the mirror. For a second Farah took in their reflections. In his eyes she was the epitome of beauty—flawless skin with innocent features. And he was athletically built, with neat dreadlocks running down his back.

Just looking at them together got people horny.

And yet something was wrong.

Where was the love?

"You're bored?" He asked.

"Exceedingly," she exhaled.

"So let's restart the Vetting process. I will double check them before bringing them home."

He didn't understand and the frustration was mounting. "My family is here, Bones. And while I appreciate you hiding Mia and Shadow out until this Baker shit blows over we're only as safe as the people you allow into the front door. Vetted or not." She paused. "I mean do you want me to leave? Because I—"

"Don't talk like that."

"You promised me fun but that part of our arrangement is missing." She paused. "If you don't want to hunt I'll go alone."

"No, hunts are always done in twos and are cancelled until further notice." He roared. "And if I find out you've disobeyed me I will never forgive you."

"Then come with me!" She said excitedly, gripping his hands and looking into his eyes. "Unless"— she separated from him and watched his reflection in the mirror— "the real reason is because you want to control me and you can do that if I taste here. Under your prying eyes."

Placing one arm around her neck he kissed her on the cheek and looked into her face from the mirror. "That's not it. I just want you to feel excited about our way of doing things. And if you're worried about the Bakers, know that I will always protect you. Do you remember the last man who tried to hurt you?"

"It's diff—"

"Do you remember?" He asked louder.

"Yes, Bones."

"Well just like I didn't allow Theo to hurt you it will be the same for anybody who comes into the mansion. And that includes a Baker. As long as you and your family stay behind these doors you will forever be safe. I put that on my life."

Farah looked away. Although she could care less about most members of the Baker family she wanted Slade to remain untouched. Luckily the prison walls were doing the job for the moment.

These days Slade was in jail for killing one of his cousin Markee's soldiers. The melee, which included the Baker Boys and Markee's men, started in Markee's apartment and found its way into the hallway.

The Baker Boys had beaten Markee's crew so badly that night that all Markee could do was lean against the wall and shake his head. Instead of begging his cousins to stop, he resorted to saying, *"Please don't kill 'em, ya'll. Don't kill 'em. They some good dudes. This going too far now."*

Slade and his brothers didn't hear a word. Although two goons were able to get away after Audio, Killa, and Major granted them freedom, Slade, on the other hand, snapped.

He held Tornado up by his shirt and repeatedly hit him in the center of the face with a closed fist. Everyone watched as Tornado's eyes rolled to the back of his head and his teeth cut into the flesh of Slade's hand. And now Slade was arrested for murder— for a case that had yet to be tried.

"Killing Bakers won't be as easy as it was with Theo," Farah said to Bones. "Theo had nobody but the Bakers have many. Just when you kill one, another comes up from Mississippi. They piling in from down south as we speak."

"Well let me—"

When they heard a scream Mia was standing in the doorway, a look of dread etched across her pudgy face. "Oh my God, Farah! I...I just got word that grandma is in trouble. The Baker Boys are waiting on her. She needs help!"

CHAPTER TWO

BONES

"Doesn't Need To Be More Trouble Than It Is Right Now."

The meager courtyard with its penny colored brick building looked too haunting to be a church and yet it was. The atmosphere took on a much darker shape when Bones and the other members of The Fold pushed open the wooden double doors.

Bones' face contorted as he took inventory of all those present for the regular Sunday worship. It didn't take him long to spot Elise, Farah's grandmother. She was sitting in the middle wearing a large yellow church crown. After the original search yielded benefits he scanned the congregation again and spotted the Baker Boys standing in the back of the church glaring his way.

Bones smiled sinisterly at Audio who was flanked by Killa and Major, Slade's brothers, along with Grant and Judge, their cousins. Also in attendance was Della Baker, the family's matriarch who looked as malicious as ever.

"Sit next to Elise," Bones whispered to Zashay and Mayoni. "I don't want anybody on the same pew as her so have everybody move."

Mayoni strutted toward Elise with Zashay next to her. An Asian and African American, their sleek frames and seductive walk seemed out of place as they nudged everybody off the bench who was next to her, causing a little controversy in the process.

Elise was embarrassed but knew what had to be done and as the congregation settled down, the pastor continued.

Bones winked at Audio, which enraged him as he tried to approach. Luckily for him Killa held him back or things would've gotten animated.

When service was over, Elise stood up and grabbed her bible. Her sexy bodyguards,

Mayoni and Zashay followed closely for protection. When Elise finally made it toward the back she gasped when she saw how many Vampires and Bakers were present. Her failing eyesight didn't allow her to see clearly before.

The back of the church looked like a war was about to ensue and she wondered if it was smart to contact Mia after all. Although she had been lying and telling her grandchildren that things were okay outside of the mansion, the Bakers had been bothering her incessantly about Farah's whereabouts and she couldn't take anymore.

She passed everyone in the aisle that were all offended by Elise's strong body odor due to her avoiding soap because of Porphyria. A rare hereditary disease in which the blood pigments hemoglobin is abnormally metabolized. The illness causes mental disturbances and extreme sensitivity of the skin to light and she and Farah suffered from it the most.

Elise advanced toward Bones, whom she'd never met although she was given slight information by Mia who told her to look for the people dressed in black hoodies with the letters 'TF' on the front pocket in red.

But somehow she knew the one with the dreadlocks belonged to Farah because of her tendency to appreciate men in charge. And he certainly looked powerful.

"You Bones?" Elise asked clutching her bible in front of her sagging breasts.

"Yes, ma'am, I am." He gazed at The Fold. "And this is my family."

Elise glared at them with disdain. Something told her *his family* was nothing but trouble for her grandchildren. "You're here...now what?"

Bones looked at the Bakers who walked out of the church but he was certain they weren't gone. "We're going to walk you to your car and follow you home if you'd allow us. I don't think things will end here."

Elise inspected him from his feet to his eyes. "You are trouble. The type of man that can get my granddaughter all tossed up." She raised her nose. "And I don't like you already."

"That maybe true, ma'am. I won't deny that. But today I'm the trouble who's coming to save your life."

Elise gasped. "Young, man—"

"Ma'am, you don't have to like me. Most mothers don't and they each have their reasons. But without me, the call you made for help would've fallen on death ears. Now I care about Farah." He gazed at his family again. "We all do. And we want to make sure you get to where you're going safely." He stepped back and pushed the church's door open. "Now can we please get on with it?"

Full of attitude, she stormed directly into the Baker huddle Della assembled in front of the building. "Elise," Della said softly. "I figured we'd meet again."

"So this is how you raise children?" Elise spat. "Huh? You tell 'em to come down on the Lord's Day and threaten an old woman?" Bones and the members of The Fold stood behind Elise like an iron wall. "I got to tell you, if this is your way of handling things no wonder they don't have no respect."

"Don't know if it make much difference. How I raise my boys that is." She eyed Bones and the vamps. "Looks like you're fully protected to me."

"Where is Farah?" Audio blurted out staring at Elise. "Huh? Where she at?"

Bones stepped forward causing Killa, Major, Grant and Judge to do the same. Now things were certainly heated. "I don't know where she is," Elise said. "And I don't want any drama from you either. Especially in front of my church." She focused back on Della. "So do yourself a favor and call off your dogs."

Della looked at her children and then at Elise. "She won't be able to hide forever. It's important she knows that."

"Whether she hides or not is her business." She adjusted her yellow hat. "She's grown. All I want is for you to leave my church. Because at this rate you got me feeling a little violent myself."

"Until next time, tell Farah we'll be waiting." Della laughed and her boys followed, all except Audio.

"Betta listen to you mother," Bones warned. "Doesn't need to be more trouble than it is right now."

"Yeah, get out of here before you get your feelings hurt, fuck boy," Lootz said staring at him. The sunlight highlighting his bleached curly hair.

Audio focused on Lootz a bit longer, careful to study each aspect of his face. Only then did he bop off.

CHAPTER THREE

AUDIO

"My Mistakes Are Mine Alone."

Audio stormed into their apartment within Platinum Lofts as members of the Baker family trailed him. When the door barred he laid into everyone like a losing coach at a Super Bowl Game. "I don't fucking get it! We had them right where we wanted them." He raised his hands and clutched them into fists. "If you ask me this family's getting soft."

"Son, you have to be careful about your rage," Della said as she took a seat at the dining room table. Killa, Major and Grant remained standing while Judge spoke to his wife, whom he was obsessed with, over the phone. "There is a time and place for every emotion and now is not the time for the type you bringing. We have to be smart."

"Then when is the time for rage? Huh?" He asked louder. "We should've snatched that bitch a long time ago and now look. She has protection and we'll—"

Killa was so close to Audio now he couldn't move or complete his sentence. Audio's body was plastered against the wall like a painting. "You better lower your voice, little man," He whispered, warm breath slamming into his face. "I think you're forgetting where you are and who you're talking to." He pointed at Della. "That's our mother. Respect!"

Audio looked at Della and stormed to the other side of the apartment to get away from his older brother. Ever since Slade was arrested and they discovered that Farah was accountable for Knox's death he was consumed with finding her whereabouts. Unfortunately, all attempts ended in loss. Defeat kept him hourly, filling any free time with thoughts of squeezing the life out of her.

And he was paying a toll so hard that the twenty something young man, looked thirty.

"What's the plan then?" Audio roared. "Because as of now ain't shit working."

"Farah is going to want to see her grandmother soon," Major said. "And when she does we're going to yank her by her roots."

"We been keeping up with that plan for almost a year, Major!" Audio yelled. "And still nothing! Meanwhile Slade in jail rotting."

"Slade being in prison don't have nothing to do with Knox or what that whore did to our brother," Killa corrected him. "He earned that body fair and we were all in the hallway to see that happen."

"It doesn't make any difference," Audio fired back. "We would've been left this fucked up town if Slade was home and our brother was alive. And now look." He raised his hands in the air and dropped them at his sides. "Mothafuckas protecting Farah and every nigga in this room letting it go down."

"Audio, nobody is about to let you declare war without a plan," Grant said. "Now I want vengeance for Knox like the next Baker but we have to be smart."

Audio frowned at all of them and felt hate. Things were moving at a snail's pace and as far as he was concerned it was time to do a little research of his own.

"Son, come here," Della said with an outstretched hand.

"Nah, ma, I'm just—"

Killa, forced him in Della's direction with a shove to the back of the head. Audio rubbed his sore dome and stood in front of his mother. "Yeah, ma."

"I know you care about your brothers," she gripped his hand, "I know you do. But you're forgetting what's kept us together for so long. Up until this moment, when we moved to DC, we never lost a member of our immediate family, while those around us have lost many. And our success is a direct result of not making hasty moves and what you're doing now feels hasty, son. You need to slow down. Before you run into a brick wall and it's too late."

Audio looked down at her and then his cousins and brothers. "I want blood, ma. And if I have to do it alone then so be it but I will have what's mine."

"Then you're making a mistake, Audio."

"My mistakes are mine alone." He stormed out of the apartment, slamming the door behind him.

Della immediately started coughing and Killa and Major ran up to comfort her. "You okay, ma?" Killa asked lovingly. "You should've let me smash his jaw for the disrespect. With a mouth that reckless the boy can handle a blow or two."

"I'll be fine, son," she placed a fist against her lips and coughed again. "Just...just get me some water." She pointed at the sink.

Judge who just ended his call, stuffed his cell phone in his pocket and went to fulfill the request while they remained attentive.

"This is the problem I have with everything, ma." Killa started. "He jumping in your face and don't even know you have cancer. How is that supposed to make us feel? It's like unconsciously he can tell you're getting weaker and taking full advantage. He would never talk that way if you were stronger."

"Weak body but not mind. There's a difference," she said.

"So why we not letting him know again?" Major asked. "Maybe that'll be the thing to slow him down."

Della drank the water and sat the glass on the table. "Have you ever heard of gasoline putting out a fire?"

"Can't say that I have," Major said.

"Me either, so why would it work now?"

CHAPTER FOUR

FARAH

"They're Looking For Me And They'll Take You As A Start."

The black and gold elaborate foyer was massive and seemed to swallow Farah, Shadow and Mia as they paced the floor. The tension was high as they waited on Bones to reappear with news on their grandmother.

"I should've gone with him," Shadow said cracking his knuckles. "Instead I'm held up in here like a bitch." He pointed at them. "If something happens to Grams..."

"Shadow, they're looking for me and they'll take you as a start," Farah said. "So the best thing you can do is keep your black ass right here." She pointed at the black and gold marble floor.

"You fit in so well here don't you?" He frowned, looking at his sister with disdain. "You got the nigga you want and the lifestyle you love. Drinking blood and shit like some weirdo."

"I'm going to leave that alone because I see you're baiting me." Farah rolled her eyes.

"Well I don't want to hear all that dumb shit."

"Shadow, let it go," Mia said. "The last thing we need to be doing is fighting with each other." She pulled down the front of her shirt, doing her best to hide her growing belly due to eating so much.

Shadow scratched his neatly cut hair and sighed. He hated waiting.

The mansion had all the trappings of a Hollywood style home, including a barbershop that he visited regularly. "It's not about letting it go, Mia. It's about realizing that at some point we can't hide forever. We have to get on with our lives. And if this nigga don't tell me that Grams okay I'm out! With or without you two."

The front door opened and Bones, followed by the rest of The Fold piled inside. Farah rushed up to him and wrapped her arms around his waist, holding him tightly. Mia and Shadow hung behind her as they braced themselves for the news. "Please...tell me she's okay," Farah begged gripping his hands. "I've been calling you like crazy but no answer."

Bones eyed her for a moment, breathing in the desperation she felt. It was intoxicating to be able to do something she couldn't— save a family member and for that he felt powerful.

"She's fine, Farah." He kissed her on the lips, causing Zashay who stood next to him to roll her eyes. "I told you I would always protect you and your family." He gazed at Mia and Shadow. "Maybe now you'll believe me."

"Thank you," Farah said happily. "Thank all of you." She eyed Zashay who folded her arms over her chest. It was clear she had an attitude.

"Not a problem...glad we could help," she whipped her red hair over her shoulder and sighed.

Mia picked up on Zashay's rigid posture even though Shadow and Farah missed it. There was nothing about the chick she was feeling.

If time could speak it would be easy to see why Zashay was so jealous. Before Farah it was Zashay who held position in Bones' life and bed. An original member of The Fold she and Bones had enough history to write a saga. She may have wanted to remember their relationship but Bones demanded that she forget, even forbidding her from telling Farah. The reasoning for summoning her to secrecy was his concern that Farah would not stay in the mansion if she were aware. To the day the only thing Farah knew was that Zashay was an original member of The Fold.

Nothing more, nothing less.

The other members of The Fold left Farah, Bones, Mia and Shadow alone in the foyer. They'd already done as much as they could for the Sunday morning and needed a rest.

Besides, vamps partied late and slept all morning. It was a way of life.

"Well did she at least accept the hotel room?" Mia asked.

"No," Bones shook his head disappointedly. "We tried but she said the same thing she always does. *'Nobody running me from my house.'*"

"Fuck," Shadow yelled wiping his hand down his face. "I can't believe she don't get what's going on in DC right now. She can't stay out there alone." He pointed at the door. "I might have to leave and watch her."

"So you think you can make grandma do anything she don't want?" Farah asked.

"Yeah, Shadow, since when did that ever happen?" Mia added.

Farah approached Shadow. "I know you want to help grandma but the chances of them hurting her are low. They would've done it by now. But *you* are another story."

"Dr. Weil just called a meeting," Mayoni said interrupting the conversation. She looked at the tense group and focused on her leader with concern. "Everything okay, Bones?"

"Yeah, I'm good."

She gazed at Farah and walked away.

Farah, Shadow, Mia and The Fold sauntered into the dining room where the chefs prepared a display of fruit in large crystal decorative bowls. Sustenance was always plentiful at the mansion, with the members believing the healthier the body the sweeter the blood.

Dr. Weil sat at the head of the table and the others perched in their regular seats. He was a character in and of himself. A handsome black man with large muscular arms, his eyes were baleful and he always looked as if he were up to something. As usual he had two beautiful women flanked alongside him wearing lipstick the color of blood.

After enjoying the delicious fruit Dr. Weil got down to business. "Now I know our line of work usually pertains to making things disappear, but this is a bit different. This client is a dirty politician who decided all of a sudden he wants into the drug game. The person he's meeting doesn't respect him so he needs muscle. This is where we come in."

"Why would he get into a business if he isn't received well?" Mayoni asked. "Seems like a foolish move to me."

"Since when do we give business consultations?" Dr. Weil snapped. "If he's paying we're working."

"Sorry, sir," Mayoni said looking down at her fingers. "You're right."

"She didn't mean it that way," Carlton said coming to the rescue. A small part of his nose was missing due to being shot in the face one night because of the beef in the street Farah had with the Bakers. Unfortunately for Carlton he was in the wrong place at the wrong time and was given a permanent disfigurement.

"I'm talking to her," Dr. Weil said forcefully. "We need this money because very soon we have to find another home. We need more space which we all can agree." He paused and looked at Bones. "Now who do you want to take with you on this job?"

Bones observed the table. "I'll grab Mayoni, Carlton, Farah, Zashay and Lootz."

"What about me?" Shadow asked, heavy with attitude. "You love picking my sister when she shouldn't even be out on the street. Remember? The point is to keep us inside the mansion right?"

"I don't think it'll be a good idea if you go," Bones said.

"I heard all that, slim, but I'm asking why Farah can go and I can't?"

"Because as long as she's with me she'll always be safe. In the mansion or out."

Shadow laughed. "This some bullshit." His fist slammed against the table.

"Shadow, please don't do this," Farah whispered. "I can stay with you here if you want. It's not that big of a deal."

"That ain't the point, sis." He yelled. "I'm tired of being in this house. All I'm saying is if he needs muscle and some eye candy to boot, you can sign me up too. Instead of treating me like a stepchild."

"Let me make this clearer, Shadow," Bones said pointing a stiff finger into the table. "You're not here to *help* us. We're here to *protect* you. Know the difference." He exhaled. "Now if you can find another solution that works I can understand. Be free. But Farah stays."

Shadow looked at Farah who remained silent. He then observed Dr. Weil and everyone else before standing up. "You know what, fuck this shit. All ya'll bloodsuckers can suck my dick." He stormed out.

Bones looked at Zashay. "Go talk to him."

She pushed back in her chair, rolled her eyes and went to fetch.

Farah was about to follow too when Dr. Weil said, "Farah, come back." She stopped at the door, looked out into the hallway and focused back on him. With a deep breath she took a seat.

"The meeting is adjourned," Dr. Weil continued.

When Bones remained Dr. Weil said, "You can leave too."

"Sure, uh, send for me if you need me." He walked over to Farah, kissed her lips and gazed at Dr. Weil before bopping out.

"Come closer, Farah." He pushed out a chair that was next to him. "I don't bite."

She smiled and obeyed.

"How are things here?"

"Sir?"

"Are you comfortable?"

"Yes, of course."

"Good, because I need you to talk to Shadow if you want to remain. Now I don't mind him staying because I know security is tough for you out in the world. But with Bones making sure things run smoothly with The Fold and business, we need as limited drama as possible in our home. In other words he's my anchor."

"I don't understand."

"I think you do." He looked into her eyes. "I treat everyone here medically because of their past mental conditions. They may look well but they suffer, even to this day, young Farah. That includes Mayoni, Carlton, Lootz, Zashay and Bones. Bad energy of any kind can throw off what we're building here. Fucking with them fucks with my money and my people and I can't have that. You understand now?"

Farah moved uncomfortably.

He was right.

She had to get Shadow under control and quickly. "Yes, sir. I do." She was about to exit when she remembered a question that troubled her since she arrived. She took a deep breath. "I have Porphyria which started my thirst for blood. But the others...how did they start?"

He laughed and leaned back in his chair. "You mean Bones didn't tell you?"

"No."

"In that case I feel honored." He folded his legs in the manly way. "When we first left Crescent Falls in my haste I didn't bring medicine for their mental conditions. It was foolish and because of it we paid a heavy price— fights among the group erupted and persistent anger. What I also noticed was the increase in headaches due to medication withdrawal." He took a sip of wine. "But headaches have always been an enigma to me because the brain has no pain receptors."

She frowned. "But I have a headache now."

He chuckled. "And I'm sure you do but what you're receiving is a message from another area of your body. All the brain is doing is transposing it as pain. You're free to

look in my library but the brain
more than a bundle of highly
nerves. This is fact. So what ca
perceived pain? A lack of blood within the
body.

"Understand that while the brain is in
"pain" for a lack of better words, blood
necessary to make the rest of the body
operate is essentially unavailable," he
continued. "So what happens if we drink
blood? That is what I sought out to find."

Farah's eyes widened.

"I started with Bones which is another
reason I value him so much. Using my own
blood I gave him one vile a day for a week. At
first I noticed his skin was highly sensitive to
touch and sunlight bothered him a bit."

Her eyebrows rose. "Like in the movies?"

"Please never use that analogy again. It's
disrespectful to vampires to be compared to
anything in the movies or fiction." He pointed
at her. "This is a scientific fact. Do the
research yourself. You give the body more

blood and it draws to muscles making it highly sensitive. In four days Bones' headaches were gone but he also developed more power."

"So he has superhero strength?"

He laughed. "Almost, except this ability is available to us all. Take the mother for instance who picks up a car off her child. This has happened many times in real life. To help her plight, blood from other parts of the body rushes to the bicep muscles to give the mother the power she needs to act." He clapped his hands together. "But if you have a constant blood supply as we do here, this feeling is available to you always. You can use it for strength or sexual prowess. It is always your choice."

"I get it now," she grinned, recalling how powerful she felt in the bedroom while drinking blood.

"We taste blood not because we can. But because we need it to feel more like who we are." He paused. "Now leave it to Bones and his sexual appetite to couple the sensation of orgasm with pain, resulting in the method we use to obtain blood today. But it is always, *always*, done so that we can be who we are born to be. Immortal." He clutched a fist.

Mayoni, Carlton and Bones were in the lounge area in Bones' bedroom, on the sofa next to the fireplace. Out of all of the rooms, with the exception of Dr. Weil's, his was the most luxurious room.

Before speaking, Mayoni took a deep breath. "Are you happy, Bones?"

Bones leaned back, looked at Carlton and Mayoni again. "What the fuck is this *really* about?"

"Easy, man," Carlton said. "All she's doing is looking—"

"But I don't want ya'll to look out for me."

"Bones, Dr. Weil has made it clear many times that the connections your parents have due to their ties in politics is the main reason we're successful and can get away with so much. If you stray than what will happen to us? We don't have anywhere else to go. It's not—"

"So this is what it's all about? My parents? I don't even see them niggas no more."

"But they're a phone call away. You know that," Mayoni persisted. "How many times have they apologized and begged your forgiveness? Dr. Weil knows that and he's using you and taking the rest of us along as sidekicks. If you leave to chase after her we all lose."

"Listen, man," Carlton started, "We know we brought her here, Bones. But I thought she would add to the experience not take from it. We figured since she resembles your ex-girlfriend, you would be happy. But it's not looking that way."

"So let me get this straight, Farah's making things worse by being with me?"

"She's making things worse because you've become undone," Mayoni continued. "I can tell in a little time you will be totally indebted to this woman and for no reason. We don't even have fun anymore! What about Shikar?"

"She's right, even the blood parties have stopped," Carlton added. "Lootz is the only one who still Trails for Givers but I heard you telling him yesterday that he couldn't bring anybody back or hunt. And it's all because of Farah. I want what we had, man. I want The Fold back."

"What is the problem?" Bones yelled, arms flaring. "Ya'll want me to be with Zashay again?"

"Of course not!" Mayoni yelled. "You never loved Zashay. I'm talking about the other one. The one that put you in Crescent Falls and drove you mad."

"Now I know you like Farah, we both do," Carlton said. "But I don't see the benefit by keeping her here anymore. Look at my face." He pointed at his nose as if anyone could miss it. "I was shot fucking with her. She's bad news."

Bones walked away and flopped on the edge of the bed. As much as he hated to admit they were right. Lately he'd been consumed with Farah and they warned him constantly to make sure things didn't go off like they did with his ex-girlfriend before Zashay.

His pushy behavior with the woman he called *Secret* was the reason he was placed in Crescent Falls, a mental institution, where he met the other members of The Fold. Back then Bones treated women as property, which he loved inflicting pain on for his personal gratification.

The last time Bones saw Secret she was brought close to death because he wrapped a tie around her neck and pulled tightly.

Luckily Secret's mother walked in and he was arrested before she was murdered.

Although Bones' parents could've gotten him help by way of outpatient therapy they chose Crescent Falls, and their heavily medicated program to hide their shame.

The rest is vamp life.

"I know ya'll care about me, I do, but if you want me to be happy that means letting me be with the woman I'm falling for," he said firmly. "I can't make it much clearer than that. You're either with me or you're not. Decide."

CHAPTER FIVE

MIA

"What Better Way To Cool A Hothead Than To Toss Him A Shot Of Pussy?"

Shadow, you have to calm the fuck down," Mia whispered harshly inside of his bedroom. "What you trying to do, get us thrown out this bitch?"

Shadow ambled toward the other side to get away from his oldest sister who was digging into his shit about his behavior. "If you think I'm gonna stay here and keep biting my tongue like I'm chewing it you don't know me, Mia." He sat on a chair he kept in the corner of the room. "I want out."

Mia flopped on the edge of the bed. "If you feel that way why you still here? They're helping you not holding you hostage. You heard the nigga Bones."

"Because I have to keep an eye on my sisters. I made a promise after Chloe died that I was going to look out for my family to dad. So that's what I'm doing."

"That's sounds all well and good but what's the real reason you snapping in there?"

He sighed and wiped his hand down his face. "I just said it. I can't stay in this place forever."

She laughed and shook her head. "Yeah, it's hard living in a house with an indoor pool, outdoor pool, bowling alley—"

"Cut it out, Mia."

"Let's not forget the unlimited access of pussy, food, money and safety at your disposal." She paused. "Shadow, we need these people right now. And even if we don't Farah does. So I'm asking for once that you think of somebody other than yourself."

"You sound stupid."

"And you must want me to slap the shit out of you," Mia snapped.

Shadow groaned. Both of them knew he could roll her under the bed, heavy weight and all, but he also respected her dotage. "I'm not about to—"

"Hey, Shadow," Zashay said hanging on the doorway. Her long cascading tresses draping her shoulders. "I've been looking all over for you. What you doing?"

Mia rolled her eyes and looked up at the ceiling. "He's talking to me. Can't you see that?"

Zashay sighed. "How about you let him tell me that for him self. He's out of pampers you know?"

Shadow rose and smiled goofily. Mia was right about some of her points, the best thing about staying at the mansion was the unlimited pussy that was constantly flung his way. And in that arena Zashay was a star. "I'm kicking it with, Mia. But what you 'bout to get into?"

"*You.*" She licked her lips. "If you let me."

"Bitch, get your dumb ass out of here," Mia said fanning her off. "You can get up with him later."

Zashay rolled her eyes and unbuttoned her blouse, revealing the top of her large breasts. "When you finish playing games with big sis, come fuck a winner. The pussy is already baked and ready." She winked. "I'll be waiting in my room but not for long."

When she left Mia stomped up to him. "You don't even see what's happening do you?" She pointed at the door.

He was still grinning. "What you talking about now?"

"Why all of a sudden that chick is so attracted to you she can't help herself?"

Shadow walked over to the mirror and smiled. "Because a nigga fine as fuck that's why."

"No, because they know you a hothead. And what better way to cool a hothead than to toss him a shot of pussy?" She paused.

"Think about it, every time you get mad you get a bitch."

He laughed. "You may be right, Mia. I can't even call it right now. What I do know is this— I'd rather get pussy than to pass the time than food." He pinched her plumpness. "You picking up every pound you lost at the Lofts. Better do something about that instead of worrying about my dick." He gripped it and walked out the room.

Naked from the waist down, Zashay attempted to catch a quick nap because she and Lootz planned to hunt later. Bones was clear that no member was allowed to Shikar until the beef with the Bakers blew over but she was good at disobeying.

Most were tiring of the tranquility that Farah's presence brought and longed for the renewed excitement. Now that Bones had Farah it was as if he didn't care about anybody and Zashay was beside herself with grief and jealousy.

She missed him.

Terribly.

Zashay was drifting off to sleep when suddenly a warm tongue trailed the middle of her ass cheeks and awakened her from her slumber. Lying on her stomach she moaned as it slid up and down before penetrating the walls of her tight asshole.

She smiled and whispered, "Now that's how you say hello."

He gripped her ass and continued to work, electing not to speak. As juicy as it felt he could go at it all night if he desired. His tongue grew pointed and wet and suddenly her pussy awoken. Placing her fingers on her clit she flipped her button repeatedly before she came sooner than she wanted.

Hearing her moan he stopped and said, "Damn you must've—"

Abruptly he was tossed face up on the bed because now it was her turn to please him.

She yanked and prodded at his jeans until his large dick stood tall before her. She hoped he'd be rough like in the past and force his dick between the plushness of her lips.

As if he could sense her desires Shadow grabbed her by the hair and tossed her on the bed so that she was face up on her back. Wasting no time, he squatted over her face and plunged his dick deep into her throat.

His aggressiveness turned her on as she slurped, squeezed and sucked him like she was rousing another orgasm for her self. Shadow fucked her face so hard that his balls slapped against her lips repeatedly until he exploded his toasty salve down her throat.

She swallowed his cream before wrestling him again until he was on his back and she was straddling him. Turned on still, she removed a razor from her bra strap preparing to slice into his waist to lap at his blood until he snatched her wrist and flipped on the lamp. "What is up with you niggas and the creepy vampire shit?"

"Come on, Shadow, let me taste it a little." She licked her lips. "I promise it will feel good."

He lifted her by the waist and tossed her next to him causing her body to bounce on the mattress. "You not about to suck my blood."

She giggled. "How is it possible that your sister, *the almighty Farah Cotton* satiates her thirst but you don't?"

"Because she's her and I'm me."

She grew serious. "Tell me, Shadow, what kind of person is Farah?" Her eyes widened. "Why does the world seem to hate her and love her at the same time?"

Shadow sat on the edge of the bed and looked down at her pretty face. He eased a finger into her mouth, followed by a second and third enjoying the feeling as she sucked them all. Gripping his dick with his other hand he said, "Damn, the mouth feels as good as that pussy."

She winked.

Abruptly, he removed his fingers and frowned. "The sex is great, Z. Some of the best I've ever had. But don't ask me about my sister 'cuz I don't trust none of you niggas in this bitch. Good sex or not."

CHAPTER SIX

AUDIO

"I'm A Grown Ass Killer."

(Days Later)

Audio was draped over the dim bar at Morgan's Night Club like his world had come to an end. Several empty glasses surrounded him and he looked as if he couldn't stand up straight if propped against a wall.

As Audio was seated he contemplated life and how things turned for the worse since arriving in Washington DC. Back home everyone was warm and inviting but on the east coast things seemed so different.

He detested the looks he drew from DC niggas when they heard his heavy country accent. Without getting to know him they'd assume he was slow and so he hid his dialect in and effort to fit in.

But fit in with whom?

And where did his adaptations get him? Nowhere!

He was growing hateful and like Slade would make a fool out of anyone if they challenged him. He desired to leave DC like yesterday but first he had to do two things. Avenge Knox's death by killing Farah and second, raise enough money to get Slade out of prison.

Across from the bar, tucked in the corner was Lootz, a member of The Fold. Unlike other members he grew tired of sexing the same people in the organization and chose to search the world for fresh blood. Policy in The Fold was clear, hunting until the beef was over was forbidden. Bones changing policy didn't take away his urge for blood.

So he decided to do something about it.

When Mercy, who was no more than 5'5 and 125 pounds, if she ate breakfast, sashayed up to him. Lootz handed her a stack of one hundred dollar bills. She opened the pile of cash and smiled. "Looks good to me."

He smacked her flat ass. "The count is always right with us. Now go get that." She winked and switched toward the back of the bar in case he was looking.

He wasn't.

Attention redirected, he was about to entertain one of the three women surrounding him when he gazed ahead and peeped Audio hanging over the bar like a drunk. The recent beef at the church made Audio's mug unforgettable and he was beyond excited.

Lootz reached for his cell phone, preparing to call 2nd in command, when he thought about it. *I can handle this shit alone. Then maybe we can start Shikar together.*

Making the decision not to call Bones was logical to him. He wanted things like they use to be and figured killing Audio, who he was certain was the ringleader in the hunt for Farah, would do the job.

When Mercy returned with the ecstasy pills Lootz paid for, he decided he wasn't interested in making any new female friends for the night. Instead he would be devoted to Audio's every move so he had to remain focused.

The moment Audio slammed a hundred dollar bill on the bar and pushed himself out of his seat, Lootz glided out of his chair also. There would be plenty time for fun and games later. First he had to handle business.

When Audio shoved out of the bar's door and stumbled to the street, Lootz couldn't believe his luck. It seemed too good to be true that Audio, a legendary Baker boy could move so carelessly in the night. Surely a man with such a large family would be protected but tonight that wasn't the case and Lootz would assume full advantage.

The ironic part was that Lootz had no real beef with the Bakers. If the truth was whispered he didn't want to be involved in frivolous matters pertaining to The Cottons. But Audio made things personal when he stepped to him at church and now Lootz considered himself fully invested in bringing the Bakers down.

Inside a half lit parking lot, Lootz was on Audio's heels as he fumbled with the keys to his car. As soon as Lootz took a few more steps young Baker boy brain would be splattered on the concrete. The thought alone got his dick hard. Carefully Lootz removed a gun from his waist and aimed. He was about to pull the trigger when Audio turned around with a weapon pointed in Lootz's direction.

Where was the drunkenness he exhibited earlier?

It was a façade.

He had eyes on him for days and now was reaping his payday.

Audio wasted no time firing and Lootz clutched his opened gut wound as he slammed to the cold ground. With watery eyes he reached up, his hand covered in his own blood. "Help me, p...please."

Instead of assistance Audio spit in his face. "I've been following you for days, nigga. Thanks for making my job easier, *fuck boy.*"

Audio was about to fire again when suddenly two men yanked him from the murder scene. It wasn't until he smelled the sweet vanilla odor from inside the truck that he realized he was in Killa's pick up.

"What the fuck you doing, man?" Killa yelled as Major shook his head in irritation in the backseat, the truck speeding down the street. "Are you trying to give DC Homicide two Baker niggas to boot?"

Audio tucked his weapon in his waist; relieved he was staring at members of his bloodline instead of the Metropolitan police.

"What it look like I was doing?" He leaned back, a smug look on his face. "Letting them niggas know we not playing."

"You sure 'bout that?" Killa asked. "Seems like you trying to get locked up to me. All out in public and shit?" He knocked on Audio's head with his knuckles. "Why you not thinking?"

"You going back to Mississippi tomorrow," Major continued pointing at him. "Fuck the dumb shit."

Audio shot a glare in his direction. "I'm telling you right now, ya'll not putting me back on no plane. I let ya'll do that before and everything went to shit when I left. I'm not the little kid ya'll use to know. I'm a grown ass killer. So get use to it."

CHAPTER SEVEN

BONES

"You Sicker Than All Of Us."

Bones was growing irritated at Zashay's fingers, which caroused his biceps as they lay on his bed. He knew when she begged him to let her suck his dick for "Old Times Sake", and he allowed her, that it would be a problem.

He was right.

Despite her lies that she could separate pleasure from love. At first he stood strong and denied her request but after being with him many times sexually she knew his hot points and activated them appropriately.

As a result he relented.

"It's time for you to leave, Zashay. I appreciate the top off but Farah is going to be done with her massage soon." He grabbed the remote off the nightstand and turned on the TV.

She shrugged. "She doesn't mind us fucking. Told me at our bar that both of you are just friends. Not to mention we fucked many times together."

He sat up and rubbed the back of his neck. "That ain't the point." He gazed at her. "I don't want her to see you in here so dip."

She forced a laugh. "Why you tripping so hard? It's not like—"

"Fuck! What's wrong with you?" he tossed the remote on the bed, stood up, and stomped across the room. "That's why I never summon you because you don't know how to leave."

"That's why you never summon me?" She frowned.

"Bounce!"

Zashay stared at him, body trembling. "You hate me." Her face flushed. "Why, Bones? Why? Before Farah I—"

"*Before Farah this, before Farah that*! When are you going to realize you not her? And that talking about her won't make shit change? I don't love you no more, Zashay. We're family. That means The Fold, but even that can change if you continue to push."

Her hands gripped her elbows. "After all this time you still haven't forgiven me. Have you?"

He shook his head and ran his fingers through his dreads. "This isn't about that, Zashay."

"Of course it is. Everything's about *that*. Why else would you choose a woman with no history over me? Huh? You don't even know if she loves you. I mean...is she...is she prettier than me? Because I can change into whatever you need."

"I don't know what you want me to say, Zashay. I...I can't tell you more than what I already have."

"Say you forgive me." She paused. "Say...say you forgive me for killing our...our baby."

Bones felt anger raging through his body and his jaw twitched. "You want me to hurt you don't you? You want me to make you cry so you can play the victim."

"No!"

"If it's not that then you want me to feel what you do...pain. Well I put our time together behind me, Zashay. I'm done with that. You can't fuck with me no more."

She scooted off the bed and walked toward him, leaving five feet between them for tension sake. "Why would I want that? All I want is for you to look at me with some love, Bones. Just an ounce. And I want you to realize that what happened to our little girl was a mistake."

"You choked her to death, Zashay." His words were calm but his breath was heavy. "You strangled her because I wouldn't spend time with you. Because Dr. Weil had me on a job that meant I wasn't home for days at a time. You got jealous of my relationship with Denny and the other women of The Fold and you lost it. All because you were a new mother and couldn't handle it."

"That's not true! She had Sudden Infant Syn—"

"Dr. Weil saw the bruises. All over her little neck."

Zashay stomped away. "Well even the doctor makes mistakes."

"What about the first baby?" His question was firm, his eyes intense. "Huh? What happened that time?"

"Bones, that's not fair because she wasn't even born." She cried. "She was in my belly and I fell down the steps! In this fuckin' house! Accidents happen you know?"

"And nobody saw it but you," he laughed. "Ironically that time I was also gone away on business. You sicker than all of us, Zashay. And you will never get pregnant with one of my children again. That's why all you can do is suck my dick." He gripped it and squeezed.

Silence.

"I bet you that felt good hurting me didn't it?" She frowned.

"I asked you to leave. You chose to stay.

And this is the result."

"I don't deserve to be treated like this!" she screamed. "I don't—"

"Cut the fucking tears. You can't get to me anymore."

"I hope she breaks your heart." She pointed at him. "I hope she causes you as much pain as you're causing me right now."

"She's not like you. Nobody is. Which is why you're alone."

"Hey, man," Carlton said entering the room. He felt the edginess and looked at Zashay whose face was beat red before focusing on Bones. "Uh...Lootz didn't come home last night. We think something's up. You heard from him yet?"

CHAPTER EIGHT

FARAH

"They're Too Broke To Be Worth Your Time Or Effort."

George Leach sat on his couch, body dripping in sweat despite the air conditioner being on arctic blast. In front of him were members of The Fold— Bones, Farah, Mayoni, Carlton, Zashay, Phoenix and Wesley.

"I know you think I'm dumb but I'm a very intelligent man," George announced to Bones." I'm brighter than most because I have the smarts to know when I need help and when to seek it." He wiped sweat off his brow with a soggy piece of tissue on his lap. "That's where you all come in."

"We don't pass judgment. We just get the job done," Bones responded.

George leaned back deeper into the sofa, leaving a damp imprint the shape of his huge body. "You must be in charge." He pointed at him.

"Nah, man. You're the boss," Bones replied with a grin. "I'm just managing my squad." He nodded to The Fold. "Now what you need from us?"

George crossed his arms over his beefy chest. "When he comes in I'll do all the talking. The rest of you can keep your eyes on him to make sure he doesn't make any sudden movements." He pointed at them individually. "The women just do your best to look intimidating and stay out the way."

Farah smirked and George focused on her.

"Something funny?" George asked.

"Not a thing," she responded.

"Now I'm not trying to offend anyone but it's a norm that most women aren't use to violence or seeing blood of any kind. So I just want you to fall back a little and try not to get rattled. The men have it."

"The ladies wouldn't be here if they weren't ready to protect," Bones said. "And whatever comes with it."

"Fair enough."

Farah remained quiet although she had seen and continued to see her share of blood and gore. She also figured whatever business he was about to have wouldn't end well because he was obviously in over his head.

Fifteen minutes later George's guest arrived at the front gate and the group retired to George's office. The visitor's men were not granted access to the premises and were told to stay out front as Bones and Wesley brought in the visitant.

But the moment Farah saw the visitant, Willie; she grew sick to her stomach and tried to step out of his line of sight. Although her direct dealings with him were few and far between, their last meeting ended with his son being killed.

Randy Gregory, Willie's only offspring, was a local drug dealer who ran a successful operation that belonged to Willie before he was incarcerated. Six years Farah's senior, Randy spoiled her rotten even purchasing her first luxury vehicle. Things were going smoothly until Willie returned home and wanted his operation back, which Randy wasn't willing to relinquish. In the end Willie connected with the Baker Boys and orchestrated the murder of his own son. And Farah, who belonged to Slade at that time, assisted in the slaying.

Willie Gregory walked further into the office after being relieved of his weapons. Taking a seat he almost stumbled when he saw Farah's beautiful face. However, the look in her eyes told him she wanted to avoid all salutations and he picked up on the notion. Instead Willie took a seat in front of George, glancing back at Farah every so often. "You have a full house don't you?" Willie asked him.

"Can't be too safe when dealing with you." He clasped his fingers together on his desk.

Willie laughed. "If you distrust me so much why invite me over?" He paused. "Surely a prestigious councilman like yourself could find something better to get into then the game."

"Wrong again," George said rubbing the sweat off of his face with a paper towel, leaving little white balls on his clammy skin. "This is it for me. In a few months I'll be voted out of office and I need my pension set when I do. The way things are going now they'll take it from me. This is where you come in."

"So you're trusting me with your future." Willie lowered his brows. "Because even with the dope you want to grip doesn't mean you're guaranteed profit."

"It means exactly that."

"And how do you figure?"

George laughed. "Not sure what any of this has to do with the product but I'll humor you." He sat back in his seat and rested his hands on his belly as the chair squeaked. "I have a few men on the street who will triple my profit from the dope. My nephew's friends. With the money I make from my moves I'll obtain more cash than all my years in public service."

"Are you sure about that?"

"Positive."

Willie shook his head. "What's to stop the men you claim are with your nephew from snatching the pack from you?" He lowered his brow. "It happens to the best of us. And with all due respect you may be successful in politics but I've seen things that would make a nigga with a harder stomach shudder."

George, who grew cranky upon witnessing the disrespect Willie was exhibiting, decided to shoot for the roots. "I may not be able to have my own son killed but I do have the stomach for the dope business." He slapped his belly, disgusting the hell out of everyone. "Now you're here because you want my money. And I am here because I need coke. Let me worry about the rest. Deal?"

Willie's neck corded and his eye twitched. "Yeah, aight."

The meeting was over and Bones and the others were headed toward the car when Willie grabbed Farah's hand softly. She pulled away from him as Bones and the others were ready to pounce. Farah extended her hand and said, "Five minutes, Bones." She didn't want him knowing all her secrets and needed the privacy.

"I'm not about to leave you with this nigga!" He pointed at him.

"Please. You can see me inside from the van."

Bones' nostrils flared. "Two minutes tops." He stomped away.

When he was out of earshot Willie said, "Give me one good reason why I shouldn't snatch you up and take you out of here?" He paused. "After all, the Bakers would pay plenty for you."

Farah laughed although quietly afraid of his threat. "Keep it original, Willie. You and I both know they're too broke to be worth your time or effort." She paused. "And if you tried to take me anywhere you'd have problems of another kind." She nodded toward the van in the front of the house where Bones was waiting and gaping in their direction. "You know that already."

Willie's smile wiped off of his face. "You love having a nigga in charge don't you?"

"I think it's the other way around." She winked. "They always want a bitch like me."

"You'll have your day soon enough, Farah Cotton." Spittle flew out of his mouth. "I'm sure of it."

She took a moment to observe his posture. "I know what this is about." She pointed at him. "You regret killing your son and you hate me for it," she smirked. "Well it's too late for all that now."

He sighed. "You don't know what you're talking about."

"The past is the past, Willie. Let the dead be. And stay away from me. That's a warning. Speaking of the dead, how's Eleanor?" Farah smirked while awaiting his reaction to hearing the name of the woman she chased around DC in an effort to conceal the secret of her murdering Knox Baker. She was also the woman that Willie kept shacked up in secret. She use to be Willie's side chick before she got hooked on the dope that inevitably snatched her life.

Willie stared daggers at Farah as if looks could annihilate.

Zashay walked up to them and said, "Bones wants to know if everything's okay, Farah?"

She looked back at the van and then Willie. "Things are great. I was just leaving."

Farah switched off and Zashay noticed how Willie watched her the entire time. "What's your story, old man?" She questioned.

He calmed himself and laughed. "Let me guess, you hate Farah Cotton as much as the free world."

"I'll just say she isn't my favorite person." She paused. "Now what do you know about her that I don't?"

"First, what of the character with the Dreads?" Willie asked. "I noticed his eyes stayed glued on her. Even as I talked to her and he watched from the van. But he doesn't appear to be looking at me now that I'm talking to you."

Zashay was uncomfortable and crossed her arms over her breasts. "He cares about her. But I think you know that already."

Willie smiled. "And you love him?"

Silence.

He laughed. "Life is such when love is involved. Look, I have a meeting to hop to but you and I may have to connect at a later date."

"And why would I participate?"

"Do you really want to go there?"

"I want an answer." She paused. "What makes you think I would be willing to help you? If you're dumb enough to enter into business with a man who shouldn't be nowhere near dope, I don't think you're very smart."

Willie frowned and tried to hide his irritation. "You'll help me because you stood in the corner like a snake and watched my interaction with Farah. You'll help because you waited patiently until I was done. And you'll help because I may be the one person who isn't afraid to kill Farah Cotton. Any more questions?"

CHAPTER NINE

AUDIO

"All I Want Is Her Life."

Behind a thick plexi glass, within an outdated Maryland federal prison, Slade held a black handset clutched in his palm as he spoke to Audio. "I can't believe this shit is finally over," Audio said excitedly. "They said the case was televised everywhere, man. On one of them CNN channels too."

"I can't believe it's over either," Slade uttered, his expression was glazed and response bland.

Audio looked away and back at his brother after taking notice of the dry manner he used in his reply. "Why you don't seem happy? We can finally put the shit behind us. Sheriff Cramer's racist ass is in prison for all the stuff he did. All because of the info Knox had on his phone. We free!"

Slade's shoulders lowered. "*We* not free. *You* are, man."

"So this is not a major step forward? Because you act like you don't care."

"I'm grateful, Audio. I am. But you'll excuse me if I don't match your excitement right now." He gazed around. "Look at me. I'm in prison and it doesn't look like I'm coming home no time soon."

"You know I ain't mean it like that. I know you not trying to be in here."

"Listen...I'm glad Sherriff Cramer got what he deserved and them other cops too. Like you said he's the reason we came out this mothafucka. And the reason our brother dead. But nothing you told me will bring Knox back."

Audio sighed and moved uneasily. "Sorry. You right." He nodded.

Slade sat back. "Any word on Farah?" His tone was flat.

He sighed. "No, them niggas she rolls with playing her close."

One eyebrow rose. "How close?"

"*Real* close."

Slade's jaw twitched. He didn't know if he was angrier that Farah moved on with Bones or that she was responsible for killing his brother. Either way he wanted to murder everybody, especially the redbone. The worst was that not a night passed where he didn't think of her. In some of his dreams he was holding her in his arms while confessing his love but in others he was squeezing the life out of her flesh.

The struggle.

The pain.

To love someone so deceitful plagued him nightly and he prayed that God would release his heart and yet it failed to happen.

At the end of the day he adored her more than he ever had before.

And he could never tell a soul.

Audio noticed his brother's tense disposition and said, "You still care don't you?"

Slade shuffled a little. "Care about what?"

Audio frowned. "That bitch."

"You don't know what you—"

"You care about her even though she killed our brother," he said through clenched teeth. "I can't believe your disloyalty."

Slade gripped the phone so tightly Audio could see it fracturing under his grasp. "When I get my hands on her I will prove to you how I feel about her. You can tell me then if it's love."

"I never said the word *love*, brother," Audio said. "But you did." He pointed at him.

When a prisoner was being taken back after his visit ended, he purposely bumped into Slade, forcing his baldhead into the glass. Enveloped in fury he popped up and gripped the man by the back of the shirt as he was being escorted away. Stronger than most, Slade was successfully able to bring his large bicep at the pit of the man's throat before squeezing air from his lungs.

The prisoner now realized expressing jealousy that his visit was over was done on the wrong dude. Slowly his victim's lips started changing shades of blue as it took two officers to pull Slade away just long enough for his victim to get one gasp of air. It was short lived because Slade was back pressing at the man's throat within seconds.

Audio could do nothing but stand at the glass and hope that his brother would make it out of the situation alive.

Finally the two C.O.'s were able to pull Slade away and whisk him toward the back. "Get me the fuck out of here, Audio!" Slade yelled. "Get me out or I'm gonna kill somebody!"

Audio slumped in the passenger seat in the prison's parking lot with Killa rehashing

Slade's vows to commit murder. Since he was the only one allowed to see him, due to everyone else being felons, including Della, Audio was forced to take the brunt of Slade's rage alone. "He can't stay in there much longer, Killa. He not gonna make it."

Killa sighed. "I know, man, and that's why I want us to divert our focus to getting him a lawyer. I got twenty for an attorney but he won't start without five more. But the other day I had to pluck from it for expenses." He moved a little in the driver's seat so he could see his kid brother clearly. "I want Farah like the next man but war is expensive. Don't forget we tagging at our savings by keeping Grant and Judge in town. At this rate we'll never get Slade out."

"So send them niggas home! Plus Judge's expenses been going up lately anyway. What's he doing that's so important?"

"First off we can't send them back right now." he paused. "Especially after you escalated things by killing that nigga. We need all eyes now, man. The moment they find Lootz more heat will come down, which means more dough going out." He exhaled. "And far as Judge's expenses rising I noticed that too. Suddenly he needs more money for food and other shit and I don't know why. Major thinks he may be kicking out to his wife back home."

"So we adding his wife to payroll now?"

"It's just a thought, Audio. It hasn't been proven yet." He paused. "To tell you the truth I wouldn't blame him if he did. We tell the man to leave his wife home to protect her and then we keep him up here for months on this caper. Which is even more reason for you to fall back."

"I don't give a fuck," Audio puffed. "Farah not about to get away with what she did to family." He wiped his hand down his face. "All I want is her life and all of this will be over."

"Would it?" He paused. "Because it seems to me like you trying to prove something."

He frowned. "Prove something to who?"

"Slade." He paused. "I think you want him to believe you as hard as him and you not, Audio. Back up and let us handle things before Bakers start dropping in this war. Be smart, Audio."

"I'm done playing smart. It's time for action."

Rushing across the sky was a thick grey cloud that looked like smoke. Standing in her front lawn, Elise pressed the side of her hand against her forehead and stared upward. "Damn." She placed her fists on her hips. "The time I get ready to mow a storm is coming."

She shook her head and turned the lawnmower on while humming her favorite gospel hymn. Sweat poured down her face and she was about to wipe it away when suddenly she felt someone menacing behind her. "You sure you want to do this, son?" She asked, without facing him. "Because it doesn't have to be this way."

Audio placed the gun to the back of her head and bit his bottom lip. "I'm positive." He paused. "Should've handed over Farah."

"You know I can't—"

Audio squeezed the trigger and watched her large body slam against the lawn mower, turning it off in the process. Blood, gut and gore everywhere.

When she was down he shot her five more times collecting his second body.

CHAPTER TEN

FARAH

"Fuck Bones."

Farah was seated at the bar within the mansion when Zashay walked in the doorway, shocked to see her alone. A few of the men of The Fold were out trying to find Lootz and she figured she'd gone with Bones because she virtually never saw Farah without him.

For a moment she quietly observed her body trying to determine why Bones wanted her so badly. After stealing a few moments it became obvious. Just looking at her sleek physique made her sick because in her mind Zashay would never measure up.

She was about to hit it back to her room when Farah turned around and saw her standing there...observing. Zashay quickly plastered a fake smile on her face and sauntered up to her.

"Hey, girl you look like you've been through it all." She placed a warm hand on Farah's back. "Everything okay?"

Of course not.

Things were terrible in Farah's world.

First the love of her life was in prison. Second Shadow's behavior had her worried that Bones would throw them out and lastly, she didn't know what future trouble running into Willie would bring her way. "I'm fine, just thinking about shit that's all."

"Are you sure?" She gently touched her back and caressed the area a little. "Because I'm a good listener. I mean, I know it doesn't seem like it sometimes but I worry about you. *A lot.*"

Farah smiled. "I'm not gonna lie. I wouldn't have thought you'd notice. The only person you seem to see is Shadow." She shook her head. "Careful, though, because I think my brother is crushing hard."

Zashay giggled because she was certain he could take or leave her. "You know how it is here, we all play well together and I'm just making him comfortable." She smiled. "But back to you, girl, is there anything I can do to make things easier? Anything at all?"

"Cut the games, Zashay. I don't know the reason but I do know you don't like me." Farah blurted out. "Let's be honest. After all, we're family right?" Farah's tone was firm and as fake as hers.

Zashay's cheeks flushed. "Who...who told you that?"

"Nobody. As a matter of fact this is the first time I mentioned it out loud." Farah sighed. "I believe in going to the source, which is why I'm bringing it to you. Besides the last thing I want to do is start trouble."

She was relieved that Bones hadn't violated her confidence by telling Farah she hated her guts. "Farah, I don't know why you feel that way. For real I love having you here. And if I didn't you would know, trust me."

Farah nodded. "I guess with time all will be revealed."

Silence.

Zashay moved uneasily. "Okay, let me say something to break the ice, maybe then you'll trust me." She paused. "The other day the old man back at George's asked me to tell Bones about a hit on your head. Said you were in love with someone named Slade and that we should turn you over for cash. Guess what I told him?"

Farah's jaw dropped. "What?"

"To get the fuck out my face."

"But...I...I don't..."

"I know you're at a loss for words. Especially since you think I hate you but you'll come to see that your impression of me is wrong. I'm many things but a hater is not one of them."

Farah gripped the beer in her hand. "Thank you for not saying anything. Especially to Bones."

She flashed a cold smile before trying to soften it a little. She despised other bitches saying Bones' name out loud. "You don't have to thank me for anything. I wasn't about to hand you over to nobody. We're family."

Farah sighed. "I'm sorry, Zashay, with everything going on I feel like there's nobody I can trust."

"I get it but I want to say something else because it needs saying." She paused. "Like I mentioned, Willie told me about the love of your life. It broke my heart that you two can't be together and if I were you I'd go see him in prison."

"But Bones would—"

"Bones would what?" she paused placing her hands on her hips. "Girl, you would be crazy to let Bones ruin your bond with your man." She waved the air. "Plus based on The Fold rules he shouldn't be trying to hem you up anyway. Only Mayoni and Carlton consummated their bond. The rest of us belong to The Fold." She lied.

"I didn't know that was a rule."

"Well it is." Zashay touched her hand. "Bones didn't say ya'll were in a relationship did he? Because he told me you were cool. I think he said he looked at you like a little sister."

Farah laughed because she was laying it one way thick. "Not sure if I can be his sister. Especially the way he fucks me."

"That's because playtime is playtime but we leave it at that. And you sound confused about seeing your man but I'm not. You better go to him while you can, Farah." She paused. "If he loves you anywhere near as much as Willie let on you'd better move now."

"Even if I wanted I could never get out of here. Bones keeps things tight and if I'm not with you guys I'm not allowed outside. So it would be—"

"I gotta tell you, all I hear is excuses. If you want the man let nothing stop you." Suddenly she grew excited. "I have an idea."

"What?"

"All I'm going to say is trust me."

Sexy black men in well hung suits and bewitching women wearing elaborate gowns filled the dim, glittery ballroom. The power group, *Young Black Real Estate Men & Friends* were having a party to celebrate the new building they purchased in downtown Washington DC, the future home to hundreds of eminent 30 something year old people. Money was in the air and just being around the pack made others in their company feel worthy.

Zashay, holding Farah's hand, stood in the doorway and observed the swarm. "Beautiful isn't it?" She said, eyes sparkling as she eyed the prospects. "I feel like a kid in a blood store."

She was wearing a tight blue dress that hid just enough of her ass cheeks while

Farah sported a black tight dress that expanded all the way to her ankles, exposing most of her cleavage for the thirst trap.

"What about Bones?" Farah asked. "And not hunting on the outside?"

She looked into her eyes. "What did you think I told you to get fly for?"

"I don't know...I just..."

"Farah, this is about us tonight. So I want you to learn these words. *Fuck Bones.*" She paused. "Now say it."

"Z, I'm not saying that shit."

"Say it!"

Farah shook her head and mumbled, "Fuck Bones."

"Good, so whenever I have an idea and you think about him I want you to remember our motto." She paused. "Fuck Bones."

The duo waltzed into the party with their clutch purses filled with gold blades held closely to their sultry bodies. In the middle of the floor the two danced seductively together as they gained attention from potential Givers and Haters. Although they were using their moves as bait they appeared uninterested in anyone else.

Their dances were highly inappropriate as they twirled and popped their hips. Not even five minutes passed before Antonio and Roman, members of the association and career dope dealers, approached the ladies from behind.

Handsome and assertive Farah and Zashay approved of the gents. For the next five songs the quartet swayed on the floor each learning the others motions, necessary for the fuck session that would go down later.

Dick rock hard, Antonio lowered his head and moved his lips close to Farah's ear. "Come on, sexy. Let me get you out of here."

Out of sight of Antonio and Roman she smiled and Zashay winked back, each indicating that it was time for blood.

A crazy thing happened at the club...Zashay and Farah realized they both desired Antonio and a plan was placed to ditch his friend.

And now, within a small room inside the *Coffee and Wine Inn*, the threesome danced on the floor slowly, completely naked. This is what Farah missed, the thrill of the hunt and she had Zashay to thank.

High off the *E* and liquor Farah decided to take things up a notch. "How about you sit over here," she said pushing Antonio to the edge of the bed. His dick was semi hard but it would be rock solid in mere minutes.

Zashay observed as Farah slithered between his legs and massaged his dick to rigidness. "Damn, sexy," Antonio said biting the corner of his bottom lip. "Shit feels good already."

She looked up at him and winked. "Just think, I haven't even tasted it yet." She moaned.

His head fell backwards as he relished the attention he was receiving. In his wet dreams he imagined that heaven was just like this. But the show wasn't over. When he glanced across the room his dick thumped when he saw Zashay gripping her breasts with one hand while the other tickled her own pussy. Adding to the exhibit she backed against the wall slid down to the floor and opened her legs wide. Offering him a clear view of her moist pink flesh.

"Who the fuck are you two?" He moaned. "I ain't never in my life seen this much sexiness at once."

Farah lowered her head and inhaled the soapy fragrance of his skin. In the past she had issues with household products but those problems were of yesterday. Being around The Fold made her stronger and with them she could do more. So the moment they entered the room, the three took a long sensuous shower together and now it was time for action.

Farah's tongue slithered along the right side of his dick and then the other. She hadn't engulfed him fully yet and the anticipation was killing him. He contemplated shoving his dick into her mouth but didn't want to ruin the mood.

"Antonio, can I ask you a question?" Farah whispered.

He gazed down at her yellow ass hiked in the air as she remained between his legs. "Anything, sexy, anything..."

She giggled. "Can I make you famous?"

He dropped his head back and said, "Yes. You can do whatever you want."

The moment the words exited her mouth Zashay crawled toward them and lowered her pussy on the top of his dick. Up and down she moved as her cream spilled along the sides of his stiffness. Her fuck game was so on point that although Farah remained hidden between his legs, he had no idea what she was doing, nor did he care.

Suddenly there was a small discomfort below the base of his penis, directly under his balls. It wasn't enough to cause pain, especially with the sex game Zashay was giving but he did take notice.

He felt himself about to cum until Farah rose, her mouth covered in blood. His eyes widened. *What was happening?* They needed to move quickly or he would be terror-stricken and Farah didn't want him to be fearful. Pain is pleasure was her motto and she wanted him to receive the message fully.

Zashay slid off of him as Farah quickly jumped onto his stiffness in her place, while fucking him harder in the process. As he observed the crimson liquid over her skin he thought he was losing his mind.

But why did it feel so good?

"You got...you got...blood on your face."

She smiled and kissed his neck. "No I don't, handsome. That ecstasy got you tripping."

Whining her hips harder, she bucked and stirred so much he figured she was right. Besides it was impossible for something to be wrong when he was enveloped in so much pleasure. Just like Farah, Zashay was now sucking as much blood from his dick as possible. Unfortunately for Antonio, he would be dead by the end of the night.

And a slice to the dorsal vein on the penis would be to blame.

Drunk and satisfied, Farah and Zashay entered the foyer of the mansion laughing. The moment they closed the door Mayoni was standing in front of them, arms crossed over her body. "Where the fuck were you two?" She yelled.

Zashay looked down and cleared her throat, wiping extra blood from the corner of her mouth. "I was just giving Farah some air." She eased her arm through Farah's, pulling her closer. "Why...what's wrong?"

Mayoni exhaled. "It's...its...Lootz, he's been murdered."

Zashay's eyes widened and she dropped to the floor sobbing, while Farah paced in place.

And just like that the entire night was a miss.

"Farah, there's more."

"What?"

Mayoni sighed and wiped her face. "Have you spoken to Mia yet?"

Farah's eyes widened. "No, uh, for what?"

Mayoni gazed at Zashay and then Farah. "It's your grandmother...she's been murdered too."

CHAPTER ELEVEN

AUDIO

"I'll Always Be A Baker. Dead Or Alive."

The Bakers' shrieking voices stirred Audio's soul as he circled the floor. Della sat on the couch quietly, bags packed at her feet. Her espresso colored skin, sweaty due to her illness taking up space inside her body. The air surrounding the family was already heavy and yet Audio added to it with his recent act.

In Audio's mind the crime was justifiable. *Smoke Farah out in any way possible.*

What he didn't take into consideration was the reaction from his family. Killing Elise caused more tension within the lineage than he envisioned and for the first time he wondered if he'd made a mistake. "So all of this is my fault now?" He paused. The kid was clueless. "They get to do what they want and we do nothing?"

Killa, Major, Judge and Grant were loading their weapons. With Lootz and Elise being murdered consecutively they were certain that The Fold was invested in the crusade now more than ever.

"You pushed the red button little nigga," Grant smirked. "Now you'll definitely get the blood you desired."

"I don't see why all of this is even necessary," Audio said eyeing the assault weapons spread along the dining room table and floor. "The beef is with Farah not, The Fold."

"Nigga, are you that fucking stupid?" Killa yelled as he wiped the fingerprints off his bullets before loading. "Or just plain selfish? You hit a gang member and an old ass lady in a month! Haven't given none of us a chance to pop shit." He pointed at the window. "Fuck wrong with you?"

"Not to mention we don't even know who these niggas are," Major added. "Outside of favoring red and black that's all the Intel we have. We got no location or direction on them people. And now this." He paused. "But you never gave a fuck did you?"

"It's not like that I—"

"Answer the fucking question!" Major yelled causing everyone to take a momentary pause. Normally it was Killa who spoke the loudest so even Della was surprised.

"I wanted her to face us," Audio said calmly, although somewhat afraid. "And what better way to make her do it than to kill that funky old bitch?" He stuffed his hands into his pockets. "If I'm guilty charge me."

"Stupid lil nigga," Major said shaking his head.

"Our family is in added danger now," Judge added. "Trust me, that move was the dumbest thing you could've done in this war. Family members are always off limits and you went and killed their Grams."

"You act like your wife is here. She down south, so she safe."

He cleared his throat. "Don't make a difference if she down there or not. Ya'll are here so it's the same to me."

"Well I don't see it that way," Audio replied plopping on the sofa.

"And that's usually the mark of a selfish nigga," Judge continued.

"You know what, leave the kid alone," Grant said. The creepy smile that always dressed his face still in place. "He moved from the heart and now we have to add to his actions." He shrugged. "Maybe this is the thing we needed to go forward."

Judge frowned. "You can't possibly think that what he did was right."

"It's not about it being right," Grant explained. "It's about what's being done now. We can't change the past. But we can make the right moves going forward."

"This won't end well," Major whispered.

"And that's why I sent for Tanoyka and Quipper," Grant continued. "They'll be up some time next week."

Killa's eyebrows rose. "You called up more cousins already?"

Grant smiled manically. "Yep. With this move we need more assistance and who handier with .45's than them?"

Killa shook his head.

"Well we not paying for the stay," Major advised. "We barely got enough paper to pay your tab now. Not to mention the piece of pie going toward Slade's attorney is getting smaller by the day."

"Don't worry, their fees are on me," Grant winked.

Della wiped her hand down her face and observed her family. This was not what she wanted. When the trip started from Mississippi her only request was to keep her sons together. And now they were further apart.

One was in prison. One was murdered and the others were walking dead men. "Audio, I want you to take a look at your family right now."

Audio sighed. "Ma, I—"

"Take a fucking look at them!" she yelled.

Audio observed his kindred.

"At the end of this war some of us won't make it and it will all be your fault, son. Are you ready to live with that kind of guilt? Because it's coming."

Audio shook his head. "I just wanted her to face us, ma. I wanted her to pay for what she did to Knox." He hadn't said a thing new which had Killa wanting to drop him.

"No, what you wanted was things your way despite Slade being in prison waiting on an attorney we can't afford. We aren't even working with Willie anymore because this thing with Farah has consumed you. That means no extra cash is coming in."

He stood up and grabbed his gun, tucking it in his waist. "Even if I have to kill them niggas one by one that's on me."

There was no getting through to him. So Killa rushed him, pushed him against the wall and lifted him off his feet by his collar. He loved plastering him against the wall for effect.

He breathed heavily into his face. "You see that woman over there?" He pointed at Della.

Audio's eyes widened and he swallowed. "Yeah, I see ma." He huffed.

"Nah, nigga, that there is my mother. She can't be yours with you moving the way you do in these streets. So let me make shit clear. If something happens to her, you as good as dead."

"Brian!" Della yelled. "That's your brother!"

"Nah, ma," Killa continued, "He need to hear this." He eyed him closely. "You ain't no Baker." He released him. "Nah, you a gunner who going for self."

Audio frowned and choked back the tears that wanted to roll. "You got it messed up, bruh." He smacked the wrinkles out of his shirt. "I'll always be a Baker," he huffed. "Dead or alive." He stormed out.

Della sighed when the door slammed. "He can't receive you now, Brian." She paused. "Needs more time to understand where he's gone wrong. And that he can't take Slade's place."

"I know, ma. But I'm getting tired of it now. I'm sick of trying to explain to that nigga why he has to stay under control. He needs to get himself together and be the grown man he proclaims." He sighed. "Forget all of that, let me help you up."

"Yeah, ma," Major added. "Your plane leaves in two hours. On everything the last place you need to be is DC, especially now."

CHAPTER TWELVE

FARAH

"I Can't Be Caged Forever."

Farah walked the last box into Shadow and Mia's new apartment in Baltimore. It was a small abode, not big enough to call a home. But who needed space when the waking hours would be consumed with getting revenge?

After Elise was murdered a week ago Shadow made a decision that he was no longer hiding under The Fold's protection. Instead he elected to enter the light and Mia agreed to go with him for retaliation support.

"That's the last box, brother," Farah smiled breathing heavily. "I don't know why you wouldn't let The Fold help. They wanted—"

"I'm done taking handouts from them," he said cutting her off. His eyes narrowed as he moved closer. "Look, I appreciate your peoples. I do. But I'm not a dame and I don't need saving. What I need is vengeance and that's all the fuck I care about these days."

Farah shook her head. "This is not smart, Shadow." She paused. "The Fold got people waiting to catch the Bakers slipping right now. Don't forget, they killed Lootz so they out for revenge too."

"Like I said, I fight my battles," Shadow said. "So do me a favor, go on back to your little soldiers because we got this over here."

Mia sighed. "So you gonna fight Farah about not moving out everyday?" Mia asked. "If so I think you're wasting time. Besides, they are after her more than us and I feel safer with her being in the mansion than out here."

"She's a traitor," Shadow said firmly knowing it would hurt.

Farah felt she couldn't breathe upon hearing those words. Part of her hesitance from leaving with Shadow was because Bones deposited into her mind daily all of the ghastly things the Bakers threatened to do to her if caught. And she believed him, not knowing that most of what he claims was all deceit.

"We've all killed in the past," Farah reminded him. "Nobody is innocent here."

His jaw twitched. "So you making excuses for them niggas murdering our Grams?" He paused, nostrils flaring. "At the end of the day the Bakers assassinated her and Slade gave the order."

Her eyes widened. "He would've never done anything like that. If this move was done, trust me when I say he didn't know anything about it. This was solo."

He chuckled. "If you really believe that put it on Chloe's soul," Shadow continued. When she didn't respond he nodded his head, having gained satisfaction. "Exactly what I thought."

Defeated, Farah plopped on the only chair in the living room. "Shadow, I know you don't think I have your back. Which is fucked up because I've never been afraid. You know me. I'm ready for anything." She looked at him and then Mia. "All I'm saying is leaving the mansion when we don't know where they are is a death wish. And whether you hate me or not I want my brother to survive."

"News flash, Farah. Them Bakers still posted up at the Platinum Lofts! The niggas moved us out!" Shadow yelled. "Roaming around like nothing happened. They think we jokes. And you know why they're so comfortable staying there?" Because they don't consider us a threat. And you know why they don't consider us a threat? Because we haven't done shit but hide for a year. We been laid up in a mansion eating coochie while these niggas out here killing our people."

"Don't lump me in with the pussy eating shit," Mia frowned. "And they only killed grandma. Please don't make it sound like they knocking Cottons off left and right."

"You know what I mean."

"Shadow, do you agree we're at war?" Farah asked.

"Been saying it from the gate."

"Then how you gonna fight without soldiers?"

Silence.

"They took Grams and somebody paying for it." He grabbed a few bills off the table and stormed out the apartment.

"They're going to kill him," Farah warned. "If we don't get a hold of him they'll bury him in the concrete."

"Don't say that," Mia exhaled. "I can't take anymore blood."

"What should I do, sister?" Farah pleaded, feeling her face flushing. "Should I stay in this apartment and fight? Or should I stay at the mansion? Because I don't know what to do right now." She could feel hives popping up over her skin.

"You're not gonna do us any good by being out here. Just you sitting here scares the hell out of me. The only reason I got some relief is because I know we're in Baltimore and the Bakers are in DC." She paused. "So please, stay where you are. I'll talk to Shadow."

Farah shook her head. "I'm thinking about going to see Slade. Maybe he can make some of this go away."

Mia sighed. "Can't say if I agree or not. I can't even say the war will stop if you do. So for real that's your call."

"It can't hurt to try right?"

Mia exhaled and stood next to her. "They took Cotton blood, Farah. And that means at least two Bakers have to fall. If a truce is called after that than so be it but not a day before."

Farah walked to the Lincoln Town Car that was waiting in front of Shadow and Mia's apartment. The driver, a white man, opened the door and she slid in back next to Bones. "Hives huh?" He softly gripped her chin and moved her head from left to right, carefully examining her face.

She nodded. "Yep."

"You always did where your feelings on your face." He paused. "How's it going in there?" He pointed at the building.

"I've seen better days."

Bones sighed. "Anything I can do?"

"You've already done enough by getting The Fold involved. Although I think Mayoni and Carlton hate me for it."

"Why you say that?"

"They brought me in, introduced me to you and now they act like they don't know me. Or even like me."

He looked out the window. "Don't worry about them. I'll talk to 'em. It's tough on everybody because Lootz is dead." He paused.

"You know you're safe as long as you stay with me right? And that the Bakers will pay for your grandmother and Lootz?"

"Yes."

"But why do I have a feeling that you don't want that?"

"Want what?" Farah asked with raised eyebrows. "Want for the people who killed my family to come to justice?"

He laughed. "Exactly."

She shook her head. "You're probably reading me wrong, Bones. I mean, I want someone to pay. But I don't want one of my siblings to be killed in the process. Look at everything that's happened so far."

Bones gazed out the window— the car hadn't moved. "Do you love him?"

"Love who?" She asked, already knowing the answer but electing to play dumb.

"Slade."

"I'm over him," she lied. "I just want—"

"He doesn't deserve you, Farah. Take a look at what he ordered from prison. The hit on your grandmother." He frowned. "What kind of man would do some shit like that?" He paused. "He blames you for killing his brother in self defense and then has the nerve to take away the only woman who loved you as a child?"

She heard what he was saying but it didn't make sense. Slade was a killer, which was evident by his current predicament. But putting a hit on her grandmother was out of character even for him.

Instead of answering she undid his jeans. "What you doing?" He asked looking at the driver and down at her.

She needed blood and at the moment Bones was it.

Focused, she placed his warm penis in her palm and pressed her lips against his dick until he was stiff. When he was so hard it wouldn't bend she lowered her head and sucked until he was pulsating.

His heavy breaths told her he was almost there so she raised her dress, pushed her pink panties to the side and placed him inside of her. No longer caring who was watching Bones gripped her waist and maneuvered her hips until he could feel himself bubbling.

Just when he was about to cum she bit down into his shoulder, nipping his flesh just a little to draw blood. She kept a blade in her bra but she was feeling more organic and went with the emotion.

That meant teeth.

Bones loved every bit of it. As he pushed into her and she sucked his liquid she felt an orgasm ease up to the surface.

Cumming at the same time, they met in ecstasy. For that one moment Farah felt an ounce of relief, her skin back clear. When she was done she looked down at him and placed her hand against his face. "I care about you. But I can't be caged forever, Bones."

"I know, so let me enjoy you for the moment."

"I don't give a fuck what you think, Zashay," Bones yelled inside of her room. "Mayoni told me you were out the other night with Farah. Where did you two go? To Shikar when I forbade you?"

"Mayoni talks too fucking much."

"Answer the question!"

"Of course we didn't hunt," she lied. "We just went to a bar to get some air that's all."

"I know what you doing and I want it to stop. She has too much going on for your games right now. Fuck you playing her so close for anyway?"

She laughed. "Let me get this straight, one minute you want us to get along and the next minute you—"

Bones gripped her throat. "Stay away from her," he said through clenched teeth as he pointed in her face. "She's mine and I don't want her poisoned with your lies."

She smiled. "Sure, Bones." Her tone sarcastic. "Whatever you say."

Zashay paced the floor in her bedroom with her cell phone pressed against her ear. When Farah finally answered she cleared her throat. "Hey, I know you having a rough day. Where are you in the mansion because I went to your room?"

Farah sighed. "The gym."

Zashay sat on the edge of the bed. "Well finish your set and get dressed." She paused. "I'm thinking Shikar."

Farah giggled. "You always did know what to say to me."

"Of course, but we have to keep this a secret."

"Consider it done."

CHAPTER THIRTEEN

FARAH

"It Will Be An Honor To Die By Your Hands."

She was nervous and had sweaty palms and a jittery heart as she saw Slade peddle out of the back of the prison. She wasn't the only one shocked. When he peeped her sitting on the other side of the plexi-glass he straightened his stance surprised to see her face. Slowly he grabbed the phone but remained silent.

Farah mashed the handset closer to her ear and awaited to hear his voice but he was mute. She would have to be first. She took a deep breath and said, "Imagine my surprise when I came for a visit and discovered you put me on your list."

Slade wiped his mouth, squeezed his chin and bit his bottom lip to preserve the anger. "I needed motivation to remind myself how much I hate you. And what better way than to see your face?"

She smiled, looked down and shook her head. "I miss you, Slade. That ain't why I'm here but it needs to be said so I figured I'd get it out the way."

He inspected her—the tight red shirt she wore dressed down with a jean jacket and recently curled hair. She was as beautiful as he remembered and looked cared for. "Then why you *really* here?"

She looked down at her hand and back at him. "Things between our families have escalated. And I'm here because I don't know how to stop them."

He leaned in closer, a frown etched on his face. "Let me get this straight, you got beef on the street and you come to the man whose brother you killed? And you expect me to help?"

"Slade—"

"I'm not your man anymore, Farah. You can't come to me for protection, especially with this shit."

She felt gut punched. "I know but—"

"I hate you for what you did to my brother and what you did to us. Every night in my cell I remind myself how I gave you my heart, only to find out you were responsible for killing my flesh and blood."

Farah was caught off guard by how candidly he threw murder and her name out on the prison phone system. She looked around and then back at him in fear.

Slade picked up on her emotion and rolled his eyes to the side before focusing on her. "This joint is a dinosaur. No updated tracking system. We can speak freely."

Farah lowered her shoulders in relief before addressing him about her murdering Knox. "Slade, it wasn't like that...I...I..."

"You could've told me the truth!" He roared. "You could've kept it real with me and I would've heard you out. But now...now..."

"So you did put the hit out on my grandmother."

He looked behind himself for C.O.'s and then back at her to be sure he heard her correctly. "What did you just say?"

"Did you kill my grandmother?" Tears rolled down her cheek.

"I'm not a monster, Farah." He said through clenched teeth. "And I'm not you." He pointed into the glass leaving his fingerprint. "So never come at me like that again."

She was relieved. "Then I guess your brothers are responsible."

"So...so you're saying that Elise is...is...gone?"

The compassion he'd shown in his eyes was genuine and she knew he wasn't capable of such horror. "Yes and that's why I'm here, Slade. Not to make your life miserable but I'm here so that nobody else dies."

Slade wiped his hand down his face. "Which of my brothers you think did it?"

"Not sure." She shrugged. "But we think it was Audio."

One eyebrow rose. "Who the fuck is *we*?"

Silence.

Slade looked away and back at her. "What did you think was going to happen?" He continued. "Huh?" His neck corded along the sides. "Did you actually believe you could kill a Baker and all would be right with the world? Is that what you assumed?"

"You have to understand, I didn't mean to hurt Knox." She clutched the phone tighter, as if doing so would make him believe her and restore the trust. "And I definitely didn't mean to hurt you."

"Bitch, I saw you covering his nose in that picture."

His breath was so heavy it fogged up the glass. If he could he would've fractured it just to lay hands. But after the fight with the inmate he lost visits for a week. It would've been longer but the CO who was there in conjunction with other witness testimony proved he was not the aggressor.

She sighed. "Slade, the pictures that Theo showed you were fake." She said softly. "They weren't real. I told you that and still you don't believe me. You wonder why I never came to you in the past and this is why. If we were on the outside and you reacted like that I would be dead."

Silence.

She rubbed her forehead. "I'm going to pay for an attorney to get you out. I owe you that."

He chuckled. "What you gonna do? Get money from that nigga I saw you with in Platinum Lofts?"

"If I have to."

"Don't waste your fucking time. I don't want money from your man."

She frowned. "It's not like that."

"Then who is he to you?"

"He's someone who...someone who helped me stay alive. While the man I love's family is out to get me." She exhaled. "You will never believe me, Slade and I'll die trying to prove it but the only man I care about is you."

He shook his head, not trying to hear her poisonous words. "Whether you pay for an attorney or not it won't stop me from squeezing the life out of you the moment I'm free." Witnessing how much he hated her made her sick to her stomach and he saw hives rise on her skin.

"If I must die it will be an honor to die by your hands."

CHAPTER FOURTEEN

FARAH

"As Many Orgies Go On In This Place."

Farah was at the bar again within the mansion rubbing her throbbing temples. Based on Dr. Weil's philosophy she needed blood.

After sneaking out earlier, walking almost a mile to the main street just to catch a cab she was drained. Each step was filled with anxiousness as she wondered if Bones would know she left the premises alone. The mansion was huge and it was easy to get lost but he played her too closely for her to do things on her own.

Every move had to be calculated.

So the moment she arrived back she slipped in her gym clothes and splashed water on her face to make it look like she was sweating. Relief struck her when she crept into Bones' room, hand towel draped around her neck, only to discover he wasn't there.

When she asked Mayoni where he was she replied, *"Out to find Bakers. Where the fuck else would he be?"* Afterwards Mayoni rolled her eyes and stomped away.

"You look like you lost your best friend," Zashay said switching into the bar to pour herself a glass of Hennessy. "And after everything we shared I think your best friend in this place is me."

Farah suppressed a grin. "Hey, Z. What you up to?"

"I thought I was gonna have to grab a drink alone." She paused. "Oh, before I forget I came by your room earlier but you weren't there." She took a sip. "Tell me... where were you, Ms. Cotton?"

Farah moved uneasily in her seat. "I was in the...the gym."

"I must say, that body is looking right," Zashay took a sip. "Naked and fully clothed." She giggled. "But the thing is...I checked for you there too and you weren't there."

Farah sighed. "I'm not sure when but I could've been in the garden. This thing with my grandmother has—"

Her brows lowered. "You know people in The Fold are talking right? Saying things have gotten worse since you've been here."

Farah inspected her closely. "And what do you think?"

"I think the worse things happen to the best of people. And I think having you here works for me because we're similar. We're both blood luster's who need to have a good time. But I'm gonna ask you again, where were you? And this time I would appreciate a little truth."

Farah looked closer and could tell she already knew the answer so she decided to be creative with her execution. "I'm gonna trust you because I need someone to talk to." She took a deep breath. "I went to see Slade like you suggested. In prison."

She grinned and covered her mouth with her fingertips. "That is such great news! And why was that so heavy to say? Always your secrets are safe with me."

She lowered her brows. "But were you following me?"

Zashay's stare ping ponged around the bar. "Let me put it this way, you're always watched, Farah. Being in The Fold means every waking moment is scrutinized. We have to know what's going on and who things are going on with at all times." She paused. "Besides, you're our first new member. Everybody else came from Crescent...you know that."

"Anybody else know? About me going to see Slade?"

"I like you. And like I said I'll never say a word."

Her temples throbbed because everything in her power said not to believe her, but she didn't tell Bones about their recent hunts together. Maybe she was trustworthy. "Sorry for not coming out with the truth right away." She sat her glass on the bar and dropped her hands in her face.

Zashay moved closer, lifted Farah's chin and looked into her eyes. Before Farah knew it she planted a plush kiss against her lips. "Want to go to the playroom?"

Her eyebrows rose. "Without Bones?"

Zashay sighed. "He's not your man, Farah. And you know our motto so what is it?"

Farah laughed. "I'm not saying it out loud."

"What is it?" She pressed moving in to tickle her.

Together they said, "*Fuck Bones.*"

"Then so be it," Zashay said.

Farah was riding Wesley's dick as he lie on the floor made with mattresses inside a space they called the playroom. *The Weeknd's* voice sounded from the speaker system as every part of Farah's body trembled. She played with Wesley sexually before but this time it felt personal and she loved the way he was handling her body.

Lying on her back to her left was Zashay, as Gregory banged into her soft flesh. When Zashay felt Farah's intense stare upon her she removed the gold razor from the pouch next to her head and slit the top of her hand before raising it high. Inspired, Farah lowered her head and slurped the sweet blood off her skin, which oozed down her throat.

On the cusp of pleasure Farah felt an orgasm brewing when she was suddenly yanked from behind, leaving Wesley's dick standing in the air.

Rage covered her when she realized the culprit was Bones. Snatching her robe she slipped it on and tied it tightly. "Bones, what are you doing?"

Wesley, Gregory and Zashay used the black silk sheets to cover their bodies as if Bones hadn't seen them naked before. The fear came because they'd never seen him react so territorial.

"Hear me loudly...she's off limits!" Bones pointed at Farah. "Now come with me!" He yanked her by the wrist and dragged her to his bedroom like dirty clothing, slamming the door behind them. "Fuck were you doing back there? Playing yourself like a whore?"

She laughed. "As many orgies go on in this place and I'm a whore?" She paused. "Bones, cut the shit and tell me what this is really about."

He paced. "So you like Wesley now? Because you can't like Wesley the way you do me, Farah. I won't allow it."

She laughed because his craziness had reached and all time high. "We were just having fun. Can you truthfully say you never played with anyone here but me?"

"No...I mean yes...but that ain't the point."

"You're coming down on me too hard and I'm not feeling it."

He moved closer. "Not feeling it, bitch I'm taking care of you!" He pointed in her face, his nail scratched the tip of her nose slightly. "What the fuck you gonna do if I kick you out on the streets? Huh? The nigga Slade's in jail and his entire family is out to kill you!" He stabbed a stiff finger into her chest. "Who else you have in this world but me?"

"You know what, fuck you and fuck this house." She pointed in his face. Storming out she bumped into Dr. Weil in the hallway. When she attempted to walk around him he grabbed her hand.

"I overheard what just happened," he said softly. "And all I can say is this...don't let anyone push you from under this veil of protection. Whether you want to believe it or not if you go now they will kill you."

She ran her hand down her face. "Why is it so important that I stay here? You don't even know me."

"Bones needs you, Farah." He placed a tuft of her hair behind her ear. "I explained that to you already. Also we've invested in you by having you here and fighting your battles." He paused. "And that means you can't leave. Ever."

CHAPTER FIFTEEN

SHADOW

"Are You Seeing What I'm Seeing?"

Shadow and Mia remained hidden in a grey stolen ford across the street from the Platinum Lofts. There was a lot of activity brewing but two men stood outside watching everyone who entered and exited. They never left post.

Although they were unassuming, even stopping to help a few elderly women who needed assistance by opening the door, they knew Bakers affiliates when they saw them.

"How you think all of this is going to end?" Shadow asked, as his eyes remained glued on the property.

Mia sighed. "You want the truth or a lie?"

He looked at her, shook his head and focused on the building again. "What the fuck I'm gonna do with a lie?"

She giggled before growing noiseless. "I don't mean to sound like the world is gonna end but nobody's stopping this clash anytime soon. They're fighting for their family and we're fighting for ours. What would you do if one of them killed your brother?"

Shadow raised his palms before dropping them in his lap. "I want blood, Mia. They killed grandma like she was a thug in the streets!" Shadow was so angry he was trembling. "She didn't deserve that shit."

"I know and trust me somebody has to pay. We just have to make sure it's the right person."

Shadow laughed. "To tell you the truth I don't give a fuck who get hit." He grabbed the rolled blunt in the console and fired it up. After taking a big pull he passed it to her. "And Farah, she gonna make me not fuck with her no more. Holding up in the mansion like a Texas slave. Since when did she get all scary and shit?"

"Are you crazy or just stupid?" Mia asked

holding the smoke into her lungs. "As many people she sliced up and you calling her afraid?"

"Whatever."

"I mean are you actually willing to give up on a family member when we're all we got? Ma dead. Pops in jail. Chloe gone. It's just the three of us now, Shadow. Don't be ignorant your whole life."

He waved her off and when a tall man treaded out of the building with purpose Shadow lowered deeper into his seat. Mia did the same. From his vantage point he witnessed the man dap up the two men standing guard in front of the building before bopping to his car. "I swear that nigga look familiar," Shadow said.

"He's a Baker," Mia nodded. "I'm sure of it."

"If he is you know what that means, we gotta tag that nigga."

Shadow eased into traffic careful to maintain his distance. "Judge!" Mia blurted out as they tailed him in a plain white van. "That's his name."

"How you remember that?"

"He's their cousin. I'm sure of it and for some reason it just popped in my head."

Before long they were on the highway leading to Baltimore. "Fuck is going on with this dude?" Shadow asked as he continued to tail him.

"I don't know but it's getting interesting."

When they finally stopped they were in a quiet suburb of Baltimore County. Judge parked the van and entered a small brick house. He was inside for fifteen minutes before stumbling outside with a beautiful light skin woman who was nine months pregnant with child. He was careful as he handled her before placing her inside the van.

Shadow looked at his sister sinisterly. "Are you seeing what I'm seeing?"

Mia laughed. "Yes brother." She grinned. "Looks like someone very special to me."

Exhausted, Shadow stumbled up the dim hallway leading to his apartment but he was stuck when he saw Della standing in the darkness alone.

How did she know where he lived?

He'd only been there for a few days.

Worried he was cornered he relieved his weapon and glanced around for Bakers but there was none in sight.

"We're alone, son."

He lowered his weapon but kept it handy. "How you know where I live?" He frowned.

"Does it matter?" She asked calmly.

Shadow appeared unruffled but he hadn't expected he'd be found so soon. "Then what you doing here?"

"I'm here to offer some kind of truce." Her hands clasped loosely behind her back. "One that would put our ordeal to an end because that's what you want right?"

Shadow laughed. "What makes you think I would believe anything you say? Huh?" He yelled. "Your people killed my fucking grandmother! An innocent woman who didn't have nothing to do with this shit."

"And they were wrong, son. And I made my opinion known with my boys." Della said seriously. "She should've been left alone but you still have family out there you care about. And getting angry won't bring your grandmother back just like it won't bring back my child." She placed a hand over her heart. "Let us not forget how this entire thing started."

Shadow sighed. "Your son don't have shit to do with me. So forgive me if I don't give a fuck."

Her jaw twitched due to his insolence. "It has everything to do with you. You're a Cotton and you're trying to avenge another

Cotton. Just like Knox was a Baker and we wanted to avenge his death."

He laughed. "Let's pretend I'm interested in whatever proposal you're about to kick. I haven't even heard it yet."

"Give us Farah Cotton and all of this will end."

Insulted, Shadow pressed his pistol against her forehead. "What's stopping me, old lady? What's stopping me from pulling this trigger right now?" Spittle flew from his mouth and slapped her in the face.

She raised her hands, cream palms facing in his direction. "There's nothing to stop you, son. As a matter of fact if you want to kill me go right ahead. After what happened to your grandmother you would be well within your rights." She closed her eyes.

Instead of sending her to meet her maker he lowered his weapon. "I'm not like the Bakers and I'm not about to kill no old ass lady. But you better get out of this hallway quick. Before I change my mind."

Annoyed, Shadow moved into his apartment and almost flew to the ceiling when he saw Farah sitting in the corner in the dark. "Fuck you doing in my crib?" His heart couldn't take all the excitement.

"I came to see you, Shadow. Where were you?"

"Don't worry about all that but you lucky as fuck. That bitch Della was just in the hallway and had you come any later shit would've changed. I saw her walk up the block and get in the passenger seat of a car so a Baker was driving her for sure."

Farah stood up. "Are you serious?"

"Yeah and like I said, what you doing here? I thought you weren't allowed out with the common folk."

"I had to come see you."

He tossed his keys on the table. "Well hurry up and tell me what you want. It's been a long day."

"Where's Mia?"

"She went to get something to eat." He paused. "And how did you get in here?"

"Come on, Shadow. You know I got a key the moment you guys rented this place."

He laughed. "Basically you saying Mia gave them to you right?"

Silence.

"Shadow, I came here to tell you, that I'm going to turn myself over to the Bakers. I've been thinking long and hard and living in the mansion not cool anymore. Plus too much is going on with Bones."

His eyes widened. "What you talking about turn yourself over? They ain't the cops."

"Just what I said. If something happened to you or Mia I wouldn't be able to take it."

Shadow observed her closely and realized she was being truthful. "You're serious aren't you?"

Silence.

"Farah, you my sister. And most of the time you make my ass itch. But there is no way I would give you to them niggas." He paused. "But, I do have a plan that just may work since you so inclined."

CHAPTER SIXTEEN

JUDGE

"My Beautiful Wife."

The wind was dangerous as Judge parked in front of a Lilliputian house he rented in Baltimore County. Rushing, he had to drop off food for his wife and head to another meting with his brother and cousins in an hour. Time was not on his side. Although the trip to Baltimore from DC could be done in forty minutes for a homegrown driver, traffic could make a foreigner more than late.

Hands filled, Judge hauled the grocery bags filled with fresh fruit and vegetables to the front door. "Baby, I'm sorry it took me so long." He yelled. "I couldn't find the fresh avocado you wanted but I picked up some other things I know you like."

He tossed the bags on the counter and opened the refrigerator, a cold fog rolled outward. "I don't want you running out for nothing today. The weather looks really bad." He paused. "If you're still tired later don't worry because I'm coming home early to make dinner." He placed the vegetables in the crisper and was almost done when he realized she hadn't answered.

"China...you heard me?" He frowned. "Don't tell me you're sleep already. I just talked to you."

He arranged the last items in the counters, stuffed the loose plastic bags in the drawer and ambled toward the living room. "China?" When he made it there things looked in order, all except a glass coffee pot sitting on the table. "Sweetheart, what I tell you about the caffeine while pregnant? That may be one of the reasons you haven't been feeling well lately."

Silence.

Something was off.

Removing his gun from his waist he aimed into the house and treaded lightly. "China,"

Judge whispered as he advanced forward, his heart quaking so heavily he could hear the thump inside his eardrums.

Once upon the bedroom door he stopped and gazed at the wood. As if doing so would allow him to see what was happening on the other side. He just left China, not even an hour and 30 minutes ago so what could be wrong so quickly?

Maybe she was sleep and didn't hear him.

Finally he took a deep breath and shoved the door open. His lungs felt as if they collapsed as he observed the horrid sight. Across the room, on the recliner, his wife lay with a bullet to the head and two to the gut. Wanting her alive, although all hope was gone, he ran toward her, wrapping his arms around her limp body.

As he held her in his arms, a piece of white paper that was clutched in her palm drifted to the floor. He picked it up and through the tears read what it said.

No More Bakers Allowed. Go back where you belong.

Judge dropped to his knees, his worst nightmare now a reality.

Judge stumbled through the Baker's apartment in zombie mode, his clothes covered in blood. "What the fuck is up with you?" Killa asked as he, Major, Grant and Audio approached with caution. "You hit?" They examined his body.

Audio looked outside and aimed his weapon, scaring the shit out of a phone technician walking down the hallway. "You ain't see shit," Audio yelled at him.

Startled, the man through his hands up in the air and said, "You ain't never lied," before zipping toward the stairs. Audio shook his head and closed and locked the door. He tucked his gun in his waist and attended to Judge.

However Judge remained silent; his eyes bloodshot red and fixed on nothing in particular.

"Fucks wrong, man?" Major pleaded. "You messing me up right now. Tell us something."

Judge trudged toward the sofa as if each steps hurt. His body low and shoulders hunched he flopped on the sofa. Gazing into his stained palms he whispered, "My...my wife."

At a snail's pace, the family inched closer. Only Killa was brave enough to sit next to him to solicit more information. "China's gonna be okay, man. I know you want to see her and the moment we take care of business you can go back down south." He looked at his brother. "Shit, all of us can."

"Yeah, bruh, we 'bout to wrap shit up in DC any day now," Grant reasoned. "Just give us a little more time."

Judge gazed up at him in a pained stare. His expression void of hope. "You don't get it...none of you...she's...she's...gone."

Major stepped back, head cocked to the right. His imagination told him he was implying death but China wasn't that type of woman. Judge met her at a library down south and she was a virgin, avoiding the streets all of her life. "What you mean gone? She left you?"

Judge's eyes grew even more feverish. "She's dead." His head dropped downward as he did his best to suppress a hard cry.

Perplexed, Killa leapt up and looked down at him like the man was mad. After all it made zero sense. "What you talking about dead? Who the fuck would kill China? She ain't that kind of chick."

Judge could barely catch his breath. "She was here, man." He ran his hands down his face. "My wife, my beautiful wife was here." He pointed at the window. "And them niggas...they got to her man. Assassinated her like a dude on the street." His hand dropped in his lap.

Grant approached his brother in anger because this chinwag was had several times in the past and he made his stance crystal. "Do not bring that woman up top, Judge," he warned. "This ain't no place for a dame you treasure that much. We at war."

So after learning he violated his counsel and moved her up anyway, he didn't know whether to steal him in the jaw or hug him for his grief. After all she was carrying his nephew too.

"What you mean she was here?" Grant asked, nostrils flaring. "I told you to keep her in Mississippi so she could be safe. You gotta let me know how she here because I'm not understanding."

"She...she was pregnant, Grant! And lonely! She kept pleading with me to bring her up, saying she would stay out the way and now this." He shook his head. "I didn't want her to be scared or alone."

"Then you should've went down there with her!" Grant roared. "You don't put her in the middle of a battlefield! We at WAR!"

Grant looked at his cousins and grieving brother and shook his head. He knew Judge was in pain but a job still needed to be done. And no matter who died at this point he was not leaving until the Cottons paid for this travesty. What was done could not be changed so now it was time for more action.

"How did she"— Grant took a deep breath— "How did it happen, Judge?"

"She was shot." Suddenly as if he remembered something he fixed his gaze onto Audio. "And this is all your fault." He aimed a bloody finger in his direction.

Audio's eyes widened and he pointed two fingers at himself. "My fault? How you figure?"

"Had you never killed that old woman this would've—"

"Judge, I feel for you," Killa interrupted. "You know I do. But what happened to your wife don't have nothing to do with the kid this time. She had no business being here and you broke procedure. Now I liked China, we all did, but if blames going out it belongs to you."

"Are you crazy?" Judge yelled. "Audio took the fight off the streets when he killed Elise." He focused back on Audio. "And now she's—"

Judge's words were halted when he leapt through his family and grabbed Audio's throat. He couldn't contain himself. When he had him on the floor he pounded his face with closed fists as everyone tried to pull him off. But there was no way to stop the strength of a man enveloped in rage, pain and loss. But if they didn't slow him down soon it was evident that Audio would be dead within minutes.

Everyone, including Grant, pulled and tugged but Judge's hold was cemented. Finally Killa broke from the pack and a second later returned with a bat that he slammed down on the top of Judge's head.

That did the trick.

The family was on pause.

Grant looked at Killa who said, "I'm sorry, man, but he was going to kill him."

Audio rubbed his throat, eyes wide having tasted a little of death. His mother warned him that one of their family members would die but he didn't think it would go down like this.

In that brief moment the family was divided. Grant on one side and the Baker brothers on the other. In that moment a question was silently being asked. Would the brothers have to kill Grant too?

When Killa's cell phone rang he removed it from his pocket and answered, the bat still clutched in his palm, his cousin in a heap on the floor. "Who is this?"

"It's Bones, from The Fold," Shadow lied. "Now we're even."

Killa watched Grant try to revive his brother but it was no use, a little brain protruded from the skull as a result of the blow. The nigga was officially dead. "Nothing about what you did was even."

"We figured you'd say that. But let me remind you that you killed two of ours, Elise and Lootz. And as a truce we are willing to give you Farah, and put this all behind us."

CHAPTER SEVENTEEN

BONES

"It Will Never Be Him."

Bones approached Farah in her room as she stuffed clothing into a duffle bag. "Going somewhere?" He asked. "If so you didn't tell me."

She quickly zipped the bag and tossed it on the floor. "You know you should really knock before entering right?" She rolled her eyes and walked around him toward her panty drawer to close it.

Bones sat on the edge of the bed and thought about the right thing to say. They hadn't spoken to each other since he pulled her out of the playroom, proving to all that his jealousy knew no bounds.

"I'm sorry about the other day, Farah. I'm sorry about a lot of shit I do when it comes to you. It's just that I can't imagine us coming this far for nothing. I care about you and want you by my side. Can't you see that?" He sighed. "Dr. Weil not extremely old but he not the youngest nigga either. When he's dead who you think gonna run this?"

"So you gonna kill him?" She said sarcastically.

"You want me to?" He asked seriously.

Silence.

His comment filled with weirdness.

"Bones, I don't want you to do anything but give me a little space. It's all I've been asking for. Yes I care about you but I made it clear when I moved here that we are just friends trying to figure each other out."

"And I want more, Farah." He paused. "Don't you see that?"

She sat next to him and placed her hand on top of his as if he were a child. She knew he cared but her heart was already occupied. And as long as Slade was alive he'd never have her in the way he desired.

In that second, just like Bones she was attempting to choose her words carefully.

With age selfishness wasn't first on her menu although it wasn't the last either. She was quite aware of what she wanted in life—Slade, Family and Blood.

Bones was not in the equation.

She knew he loved her and she appreciated all he'd done but she needed time. "My grandmother is dead."

"And so is Lootz."

"I know and I'm sorry, Bones. But I have to help my family fight this war."

His hands formed a steeple as he tried to calm himself instead of smacking the shit out of her. "Why, Farah? We've been cruising the streets looking for them niggas for the past few days. Even been trying to gain entrance into Platinum Lofts, which has proven difficult. But given some time they will make a mistake. I'm going to—"

"I can't stay here, Bones. I made a promise to Shadow and in the next few days I'm going to make good on it. Now I know you don't understand and I can't explain more than I already have. You have The Fold but all I got is Mia and Shadow. Don't you see that?"

"You can't leave."

"I can and I will." She paused. "And you need to let Dr. Weil know my decision too because he threatened me."

He shook his head and waved the air. "He just wants me to be happy and he knows you're safety is a part of that." Bones turned his body toward her. "I can't help but feel like if I was Slade you wouldn't give me this much trouble."

"But you're not Slade." She placed her hand on the side of his face. "You're Bones and I love that about you."

He shook his head and stomped across the room. "So nothing I do will make you look at me the way you do him?"

"How do you know how I look at him? Everything about you two are different."

"I saw you once at Platinum Lofts." His gaze was glassy as he looked at nothing in particular in the room. His neck corded as jealousy consumed every vein in his body. "The day I walked you to your apartment and he was in the hallway." He blinked and moved toward her. "Farah, I will help you but you can never be with Slade. Ever. Even if you're not with me it will never be him." That was the largest threat he ever made.

Farah was growing irritated. "He's in jail anyway, Bones."

He backed away. "So you've gone to see him?"

She cleared her throat. "No, for what?"

"How come I don't believe you?"

Farah's temples throbbed and she suddenly craved blood. "I can't do this with you anymore. And I can't disrespect your home either. Like I said, I'm leaving in a few days whether you want me to or not. I'm sorry."

As she walked toward the door Zashay entered. She noticed Farah's tight expression and said, "Hey, girl. Everything okay?" Zashay was holding a grey duffle bag.

Farah looked at Bones and back at Zashay. "I have to go. I'll talk to you later." She stormed out without another word.

Zashay sighed when she left and walked deeper into the room. "Here's the final payment from George. Want me to put it in the safe?"

"You don't have the code." Losing Farah caused him great irritation and Zashay's voice annoyed the fuck out of him in that moment.

"Maybe you should give it to me then," she said playfully. "Besides, if I wanted to steal a few stacks I would've done it already. After all, I did pick it up."

"Never play with me like that," he said pointing at her.

"I'm sorry," she whispered looking at the floor.

Bones bopped toward her, snatched the bag and flung it on top of Farah's dresser like trash.

"I see you aren't in the mood." She sighed.

"So what happened just now?"

"Leave it alone."

"I'm not here to make trouble. I may not be the love of your life but you are still mine." She sat on the bed and crossed her legs. "Can I do anything to make you feel better?" She licked her lips. "Anything at all?" She removed a blade from her bra strap and hovered it over her skin. "Thirsty?"

"Why did you take Farah to the playroom that night?"

She rolled her eyes, stuffed her blade back in the pocket of her bra and sighed. "Because we wanted to have fun," she joked. "I don't know why you're so surprised. She's a blood fiend like the rest of us. Or didn't you realize it?"

"Of course I know she's like us but not in the way you making out." He frowned. "Wesley had his dick all in her like she belonged to him or something."

"She doesn't belong to you either."

"BUT SHE DOES!"

Zashay laughed, totally embarrassed. "You know what, maybe you should lighten up a little. I'm starting to think she isn't as bad as I believed. Maybe the real problem is you."

"Don't talk to me about anything pertaining to Farah." He paused. "And most of all, stay away from her. Whatever this friendship you built is, I want it to end today." He pointed at the floor.

She walked over to Bones and grabbed his hand. "You have disconnected from family, Bones and we need you back. That's all I want for us. If ending my friendship with Farah is what you desire than it's done. But will you end your friendship with her too?"

Silence.

"It's amazing how some women will do anything to get the nigga they want, even fake befriend the other bitch."

Insulted she moved toward the door and he grabbed her before she exited. "Let go,

Bones. If you don't want me than I'm starting to think that maybe that isn't such a bad idea." She was staring to sicken of his shit.

He held her hand and squeezed tightly. She wasn't the woman he craved but there was something that could be said about her beauty and her tenacity to prove her adoration. "Do you love me?"

"Always, Bones that will never change."

"Then keep an eye on her, Zashay." He grabbed her shoulders and massaged them lightly. "Let me know what she does every minute of the day. If you do this, it will prove to me how much you care and I will show my gratitude."

CHAPTER EIGHTEEN

AUDIO

"No More War."

Perched in front of Slade on a visit, Audio could tell by his stiff disposition that something was wrong. "We talked to an attorney but he wanted more money than we got right now," Audio advised. "But Killa hit up a poker game last night and made five thousand but we need five more."

Slade laughed.

"What's funny? At least we're trying to get you out of here."

Slade rubbed the back of his head and dropped his hand on the table. "I'm gonna be honest, kid, I'm bracing myself for the long haul. Whether you get an attorney or not is up to you. Doesn't seem like I'm getting out anytime soon."

He frowned. "It's not like we don't have time, Slade. Your case is in a month."

"And I expect to get a public defender who doesn't know shit or give a fuck. Even with Sherriff Cramer being arrested, the laws in this place still believe I killed an officer. And they treat me accordingly." He exhaled. "I want you and the family to go back home. Tonight. Let me deal with this up here alone."

"So that's what this is about? You want us to leave a Baker on the field?"

"I can't have anybody else get hurt, Audio. Go home. Take Major and Killa with you."

Audio shook his head, looked down at the desk and back at him. "I'm sorry, man. But there's no way I'm leaving you in this cage. I know you doing the honor thing by wanting us down south and all but it ain't happening."

"What's been going on out there, Audio? Huh? What's been happening with the family?"

The question was asked but it was obvious he already knew the answer. "Oh, you talking about that thing with China. Something happened with Judge's wife...she was—"

"What fucking happened?" He roared so loudly Audio thought he was on his side of the glass.

Hearing the noise a guard advanced toward Slade. "One more like that and it's over. This time your visits won't be reinstated....BAKER. I'll see to it." He frowned and stormed away.

Audio shifted in his seat and cleared his throat. "They got China and an accident happened with Judge."

Slade exhaled deeply, his day already ruined. "How did it happen, Audio? What you do now because I know you were involved? Huh, man? What beef did you chase that resulted in all of this?" He squeezed the handset tighter.

"Nothing, man." He shrugged. "This time it was outside of me. The Fold got her—"

"And what about Judge?"

Audio took a deep breath. "Killa got him with a bat when he was on me." He turned away from Slade's glare finding it difficult to come clean to his oldest brother. "He's gone, man. I'm sorry."

Slade's eyes widened. "Are you happy now?" A tear rolled down his face and it was the first time Audio had seen his brother cry. And if God was willing he hoped he'd never have to see it again.

"By doing Elise you let it be known that no family member is off limit," Slade continued. "You did this shit, man. You!" He pointed at the glass. "Not only did you move without thinking you did it while I'm in here, unable to help my family."

"I know you mad but the niggas would've done it to ma if they had a chance." He paused. "I don't feel all that guilty about that part."

A boisterous sinister laughed exited Slade's gaping mouth. "You don't know do you? You have no idea?"

Audio moved uneasily in his seat. "What you talking about?"

"Ma found out where the nigga Shadow lived in Baltimore, before he moved again."

"When was this?"

"It don't matter. Just know that she stepped to him to call a truce if they handed over Farah. Shadow had the chance to kill her then, even whipped a gun out but he didn't. I think she wanted to die. He spared her life unlike what you did to Elise."

His eyes widened and he scratched his head. "Ma didn't say anything to me about all that."

"You know what else ma didn't tell you? That she's dying. Cancer eating her breasts and she don't have many more months to live. Nobody wanted to tell you because they wanted to spare you but fuck you and your feelings, lil' nigga." He pointed at the glass. "You deserve to be burdened with as much pain as the rest of us."

Audio felt sick and the room felt like it was spinning. "Ma...ma's dying?"

Silence.

"But, she...I..."

"Now you want your mommy?" He chuckled angrily. "I told you when we first got to DC to chill out," Slade whispered. "I begged you to slow down because she been sick for a long time. Before we got here I told you we needed to do the job and leave. But you were dead set on showing niggas you weren't slow just because of your accent. You wanted to do more to prove you were tough and now look around. All we left with is suffering."

Audio felt weak but he didn't want to express his pain. He'd been so disrespectful to his mother with his plight to get at Farah that he felt he exacerbated her illness.

Slade was right.

They lost so much and at the same time there was no turning back. Even Grant agreed to put his brother's murder to the side although Audio knew when it was all said and done that Grant would kill him next.

These days it was as if they were driving through a dark tunnel with no headlights. They couldn't stop because they could get hit and the only way was forward. "Slade, I'm—"

"There's nothing you can say to make me forgive you. The shit you did means all of us suffer. Should've let me deal with Farah alone like I begged." He stood up. "If my mother dies while I'm in here you gonna see me soon, lil nigga. And not even this cage will hold me." His nostrils flared. "Don't come back, Audio. Ever." He hung up the phone and stomped away.

Audio sat in his car outside of the prison with the phone glued to his ear, his mother's voice on the other end. "Things will be okay, Audio." She coughed. "Trust me."

"But I didn't know, ma. Why you never told me you were sick?"

Della sighed. "Because that information wasn't for you. And I wish my oldest hadn't told you now." She paused. "But like Grant said what's done is done."

Audio felt a wave of emotion bubbling at the surface and he forced it down. He couldn't lose his mother. He just couldn't. Crying would make him appear weak and cause his mother additional pain, something he'd done enough of already. "Ma, I'm sorry. I should've never disrespected—"

"Son, you don't have to do this."

"I do, ma." He exhaled. "I put this family through a lot and I want you to know that I'm going to make things right." He looked around and pressed his head against the headrest. "I can't imagine life without you."

"Then don't. And if God's willing you won't." She paused. "I'm in chemotherapy right now, son. At first I wasn't about the fight because I didn't have the strength. But I know Slade would never forgive himself if I died while he's in that cage. Maybe there's something too this white people medicine after all." She giggled. "If so I'm going to find out."

Audio sighed. "I'm gonna make sure this mess is wrapped up in DC, ma. No more war."

"Son, the war is already started. Now it's time to finish without spilling any more Baker blood."

CHAPTER NINETEEN

AUDIO

"I'm From The Bottom."

Standing in a corner, doing his best to appear incognito, Audio concentrated while his family went over the details for plucking Farah off the street, despite The Fold's claim to hand her over willingly.

As more points rolled out about the plan to meet them in a secret location were revealed, Audio sensed something dark was about to happen to his people. After promising his mother that he would stop Baker blood from spilling he felt responsible for saying his piece.

"Am I the only one who thinks this a set up?" Audio asked as he walked away from the corner and plopped next to Major and Killa on the sofa.

Grant stood in front of them, his eyes bearing down on Audio with distaste. It was obvious Grant hated him with a passion and had plans to deal with Audio later but first it was all about the Cottons and The Fold.

"You don't think we know that?" Grant asked, his tone much snappier than in the past. "Listen, do us a favor and let us handle the details. You've done enough already." Having to bury his brother plagued Grant consistently. China being in town may not have been Audio's fault but killing Elise was the fuel that inspired his murder.

"I'm just asking that we think things through a little more."

"Like I said I know what we doing," Grant continued extending his palm so that it was near his nostrils. "But we have something for them niggas too."

"And I bet you they have something for us."

Major laughed. "Now that two niggas done died on a count of you, you wanna play smarter?" He chuckled. "Forgive us if we aren't hearing you right now."

Audio sighed. "I made a mistake and I'm realizing that now. But it could've taken me longer." He looked at his family. He was being sincere but they wanted him as far away from the plan as possible. "But I'm not about to sit in this circle without saying something, whether ya'll mad at me or not."

"Little nigga, nobody feeling you," Grant continued. "Now shut up and let us work out this plan."

"You know what, fuck it. I'll put into motion my own shit." He hopped up and grabbed his keys.

"If you do something else that brings more drama on this family you cut," Killa warned pointing at him. "You done used up all your strikes. You have nothing left. In a minute not even we'll be here for you."

Audio cruised down the street pumping Tupac's greatest hits. His temples throbbed as he recalled his solecisms and realized he would make many more in the future. He was unsophisticated and moved at maximum speed when things didn't go his way but his heart was mostly in the right place, especially now.

There was another issue plaguing him on a regular that he didn't share with the family. And it was that he never got over the love of his life—Chloe Cotton.

Like Slade he fell for a Cotton the moment he touched D.C. soil and she was taken from him suddenly in a car accident. One minute he was realizing his feelings for her and the next she was dead and he never got a chance to grieve, blaming Farah like everyone else for his loss.

As the music pumped through the speakers his aspirations about Slade and how he let him down played on repeat in his mind. He had to think hard on what needed to happen to bring things to a smooth end. There were so many unanswered questions.

Who was The Fold?

Were they a gang or something deeper?

Who did they represent?

And how powerful were they?

When the wheels began to churn he remembered something important. But he had to move quickly.

Within the darkness of Morgan's Night Club, Audio deposited himself in a chocolate brown leather seat in VIP. His gaze was fixed on the cutie who Lootz visited the night he murdered him. Since the police were actively investigating the crime for suspects, which wielded no new leads, he had to be cautious.

When the cutie sashayed toward him, a grin sitting on her face, he decided to lie on the charm Mississippi men were known for. Sure his accent was different and lent enough material for immature easterner's to find comedy. But there was one problem, many women on the coast were lonely and for a broken heart what better cure than a southern gentleman?

"Have you been helped, handsome?" she flirted before winking. "Because I'm here to serve."

Audio adjusted his black baseball cap allowing just enough of the strobe lights to caress his dark chocolate skin. "I haven't been helped. Not properly anyway." She smiled and Audio knew she was under his spell.

She flipped her long black weave over her shoulder as if he couldn't see it hanging in the back. "What's that supposed to mean?"

"I'ma be honest, it means whatever you want it to." He found himself applying a heavier accent, unknowingly making a silent vow to rep his set.

"You not from around here are you?"

"I'm from the bottom, then again you probably knew that already."

She smiled wider. "Why you look so familiar?" She pointed at him. "You been here before?"

"Nah." Audio's stomach bubbled and he pulled his cap down a little, afraid she would have total recall from the night of Lootz's demise. "Doubt you know me but we can rectify that if you desire."

"Rectify huh?"

He winked.

"So how we do that?" she asked.

"For starters, let's get the fuck out of here."

"Now I don't want to hurt you," Audio explained as he aimed a .45 at the pretty girl, who he now knew as Tomi, nickname Mercy. She was so light skin she could pass for white but at the moment her skin was crimson.

"I can't tell," She trembled. "Because right now it looks like you want to kill me. What do you want?"

Audio turned his cap toward the back. "Some time ago you were entertaining a nigga wearing black and red. Matter of fact that's all he ever wears...black and red."

"The one who was murdered?"

"Yes."

"You were there that night," she mistakenly pointed at him. "I remember you now...at the bar."

He shook his head. "I wish you never said that. I really do."

She covered her mouth with her fingertips realizing her mistake may cause her life. At least now she knew what he wanted. "I knew him...well kinda."

"How?"

"They have private parties at a mansion that's off the grid. You have to go through hell to get invited and even then there's a gate that circles the entire property."

"Who the fuck are they?" Audio asked. "Drug dealers?"

Her eyes widened. "Wait, you really don't know? You really must not be from DC."

Silence.

"They're vampires. Well...not in the traditional sense. They crave blood and host elaborate parties to lure people. Now they don't bite or anything like that. It's nothing like you see on TV because they use razors instead of teeth. Slits." She raised the sleeve of her dress and showed him her arm. Embedded on her skin were several pinkish raised marks.

"Fuck is that?" He frowned.

"Cuts, from when they tore into my skin. It didn't hurt especially with the ecstasy. To be honest there's something erotic about how they do it that I can't explain. As they're cutting you want more because you can't get enough."

He noticed how a slight smile spread on her face and her left leg rocked as if she was trying not to piss on herself.

"That's what you keep in the back of the bar?" He paused. "X?"

She nodded. "It's not mine. The owner makes the deals and I just bring the stuff to his clients."

"Since they host parties that means they don't care who knows where they live." He reasoned.

"Far from the truth," she corrected him. "They never allow people to know where they live. To come and go they give you some kind of sweet drink, tastes like grape Kool-Aid but I don't know what it is really." She paused. "Anyway the drink must be laced with something, probably Rohypnol but I'm not sure. All I know is they pick the people they want, buy them the drink at the bar and when they wake up their in the mansion."

"Why bring them to their house though?"

She shrugged. "Not really sure about that either. I think they give on site infection tests because one time when I woke up I had cotton in my mouth. Like from a swab or something."

He laughed. "So these creeps drink blood and giving out HIV tests?"

"I don't know what they give out I'm just assuming. What I do know is that it's always a good time in the mansion and the people they pick are theirs for the weekend. Food, liquor, a pool, a bar, a bowling alley, you name it and it's in that house. It's a pleasure being with them if I'm being honest." She smiled and her leg rocked again. "Very seductive." She gazed into the night.

"So you're no use to me since you don't know where they live."

Her eyes widened. "I never said *I* don't know where they live." She paused. "Rohypnol has no effect on me. Never has. Maybe it's because I suffer from something called Anesthesia Awareness and can't even go under when given general anesthesia before surgery. All I know is that I was awake on the way to the mansion. And I was awake when we were driven out."

Slowly Audio pulled next to the trees surrounding the mansion, some feet away from the iron wrought gate. He was close enough to see the house but not be detected on their cameras. From his viewpoint he was amazed at all of the beautiful black people in big luxury cars that entered and exited the premises.

He could certainly see the appeal.

"You're in there Farah. Aren't you?" He said to himself.

After observing a bit more he knew it was time to leave, fearful he would be spotted.

"Sorry I did that too you, Tomi," Audio said as his eyes remained glued on the residence. "But with this info I can get my family out of a bind. Because now at least we know where they lay their heads."

He looked in the passenger seat at Tomi who was already dead after he delivered a bullet to her gut. "It's just too bad I had to kill you in the process."

CHAPTER TWENTY

FARAH

"I Can Remember Like It Was Yesterday."

The members of The Fold were convened around the dining room table as they listened to Dr. Weil boast of profits gained from their recent ventures. He was flanked to his left and right by members of The Fold and appeared certain that good things were coming their way.

With a glass of wine raised in the air he said, "There's no denying that we're worth more than ever. And I'm calling this meeting to announce that I've purchased a new property in Delaware that we will be relocating too shortly."

Everyone sighed. "Sir, but why?" Mayoni asked, Carlton sitting at her side. "I thought when you purchased this property you said it would be forever."

"I made a mistake and we talked about that in the last meeting." He paused. "Besides, we've gained some unwanted attention and I think it's time to relocate. Nothing is forever, Mayoni."

Quiet whispers filled the room.

"But, sir, this is home," Carlton continued, worried Mayoni was on the verge of a nervous breakdown. "Are we sure this is the right move for the family now?"

His fears for Mayoni's mental condition were warranted. After being left in an orphanage in Korea, and adopted in America, only to be left again, Mayoni suffered from fear of abandonment. This was also one of the reasons she was admitted into Crescent Meadows and placed under care. When Dr. Weil helped them escape he represented stability and she needed that trait for peace of mind.

Essentially she hated major changes.

"It's happening. We moving," Dr. Weil announced happily.

"All I'm saying is why so soon?" Mayoni pleaded. "I thought we'd have more time."

Dr. Weil cleared his throat. "I think you need to remember something, beautiful, this is my organization and—"

"No!" Carlton yelled bringing his fist down on the table, rattling plates and silverware. "This is all of ours! You may have helped us escape but you did not build this business alone."

Bones rose to his feet and pointed at Carlton, causing him to settle down quickly. "If we must leave then we must. Arguing about it won't stop it from happening, besides, the paperwork has already been signed."

Mayoni frowned. "So you knew about this? And didn't tell me?"

"He knows everything," Dr. Weil added.

"I have an announcement to make too," Farah interrupted. "I'll be leaving in a day or so. I know my trouble on the streets has inspired this move and I think it will be best if I left."

"But Farah, you heard what Dr. Weil said," Bones responded. "Nothing is forever." He grabbed her hand and she wiggled out of his clutch.

"Let her go, Bones," Mayoni pleaded. "It'll be best for us all."

"She's right," Carlton added. "Let's put it to a vote. Who here wants to see Farah gone?"

The members shuffled a little and one by one everyone but Dr. Weil, Bones and Zashay raised their hands. "Well, it's unanimous. She has to leave immediately."

Being voted out hurt but Farah understood.

"I will never forgive you for what you just did," Bones said to Mayoni. "You will remember this."

Tears rolled down Mayoni's cheek. "Listen to me, I know you care about her. I have a soft spot in my heart for Farah too." She gazed up at Farah. "But this is too much. We have to let her make her own mistakes. Now we supported you in the beginning but look what it has gotten us? Lootz killed. Who must die next before you choose us?"

"So we have to let her go," Carlton added. "It's the only way."

"It's not that easy," Bones continued as if Farah weren't present.

"Why not, brother?"

"Because if she goes I will too."

Farah looked down at him. "Please don't do this."

"I'm not going to stand by and watch this," Mayoni wiped her mouth with the white linen napkin and rose. "If you want her instead of The Fold then so be it." She exited with Carlton following.

Bones tried to find Farah in the mansion but when he couldn't he retreated to his room. As always Zashay followed. "You're making a fool of yourself."

He laughed sarcastically. "Let it go, Zashay."

"I won't! You asked me to follow that bitch and now you're willing to leave if she does? Causing the family to take it to a vote. What is happening to you? You're tearing us a part for a woman who doesn't give a fuck about you or us." She dropped to her knees. "Not like I do." She kissed his feet.

Farah who was in the doorway moved deeper into Bones' room upon seeing the performance. She focused on Zashay who stood up and brushed her knees.

"You should've stayed down there where you belong, snake."

"Farah, I was just playing with Bones," Zashay smiled, wiping tears from her face. "How long were you there?"

"Long enough to see all I needed to." Farah laughed. "If I ever catch you on the street I will open up your throat," she said to Zashay. "Remember that."

Bones stepped. "Farah—"

Stay the fuck away from me," she yelled pointing at him. "Both of you!"

Farah walked into Mayoni's room who was sitting on her bed sipping a glass of blood colored red wine. "I bet you can't remember the day you first met me," Farah said playfully.

Mayoni smiled partially, still devastated at the upcoming move. "Yes I do. You were coming out of Platinum Lofts and this dude approached you, angry over something you did." She shook her head. "I must say, trouble always follows you doesn't it?"

"Wrong," Farah corrected her with a smile. "Not about the trouble but the other part."

Mayoni searched her mind. "No, that was it. I can remember like it was yesterday."

"I can too. It was the day that changed my life forever." She sat next to Mayoni. "But our meeting occurred on an elevator. You were with Carlton and I thought you were as beautiful then as you are now."

Mayoni laughed. "While I appreciate the compliment we were outside your building. I'm sure of it. And I asked, "Are you Farah Cotton?" She paused. "And you said...."

"*Who's asking*?" they both said together.

Now Farah remembered.

They giggled before simmering down. Mayoni was right and she was wrong. "I'm sorry I caused you so much pain, Mayoni. And I want you to know no matter what I appreciate everything you've done for me."

"So you really are leaving?"

"Yes."

She nodded. "Is it because of Slade?"

Silence.

"Be decent and tell me the truth, Farah. After everything I have a right to know."

Farah sighed and held her hand. "I have never and will never love a man more than I love him, Mayoni. It's impossible. I know we can never be together but I won't be happy with anyone else if he's not at least safe." She squeezed her hand a little harder. "I'm sorry for hurting Bones and I hope you understand. It was not my intent."

Mayoni exhaled. "Take care of yourself, Farah. And thank you for letting Bones go."

Mayoni was brushing her hair when Dr. Weil slid into her room, closing the door. He stuffed his hands deeply into his pockets and walked toward her. "He can't leave."

"Sir?" Her eyebrows rose.

"Bones. If he leaves all of this goes away." He raised his hands and turned around the room. "Do you know where this Slade is?"

"I do sir. He's in prison."

"Find a way to kill him. If you kill the man she will have no choice but to come to him."

"Sir—"

"Let me make this clearer. Bones can't leave under any circumstance. See to it that doesn't happen."

Farah was on her feet again.

Since the plan was to give herself over to the Bakers she wanted to have one last hunt for old time Shikar. If she was going to die she needed to make sure her last days were filled with her desires.

K. Michelle's voice boomed from the speakers as she glided down the highway, the night sky dark purple. Driving a rental, her mind was on Slade and what never became of their lives together. Touching her belly she imagined how it would have felt to have his seed inside of her, a bestowal she would never realize.

Tears rolled down her face and were blinding as her thoughts roamed. What kind of mother could she possibly be when the quest for the hunt was more important than life? She was drawn to risky behavior, sexually and mentally and there was no way out but quietus.

Wiping the tears from her eyes she decided to speak to the Man on High. Something she'd rarely done. "God, if I'm not supposed to be who I am please take this urge away from my—"

THWACK.

Her eyes widened, as she was jolted forward by a thunderous racket. She wondered where it stemmed from as she gazed through the rear view mirror. No one was behind her so what occurred? Pulling to the side of the road she parked eased out and ascertained the damage.

It was a flat tire.

"Fuck!" She called out into the night.

When a set of headlights drew nearer, a detailed white Cadillac Escalade eased behind her car and parked. Seconds later a 6 foot 4 inch Adonis, with butter brown skin, covered mostly in tats, exited the vehicle. A black Kufi sat on top of his raven colored hair that was pulled into a long ponytail.

She'd never seen anything like him in her entire life.

Was he black or Pakistani? She couldn't be sure. What she did recognize was his perfection. His presence filled up the space, similar to Slade but different. It was obvious that this man was loved upon.

He was also an alpha male.

"Trouble?" He asked examining the blown tire.

"Not anymore," Farah said, wondering how sweet his blood would taste.

Considering her response he investigated her long and hard. Chemistry was brewing between them and it was as if they were created from the same pen. "You want to get out of here then?"

She grinned. "If you'll have me I guess I'm coming with you."

As Farah sat in his car she thought about the silent prayer she was making before the tire blew. *"God, if I'm not supposed to be who I am please take this urge away from my soul,"* was what she wanted to say.

Unfortunately her personal demons answered first and brought the sexy blood bag her way.

"By the way, the name's Rasim," He said steering the truck down the road, deeper into the night. "What do they call you?"

"Farah," she whispered. "Farah Cotton."

This wasn't supposed to be the plan but making love to him felt so right. There was something to be said about being fucked by a man sitting on a chair, his body under hers, as he pumped into her hot flesh. Even still this fuck session was different. She got the impression that Rasim made lovemaking an art which as why she hadn't tasted his blood. Farah wanted to witness the experience, allowing it to last a bit longer than in the past. She was still wearing her bra waiting for the perfect moment to cut and yet it had not happened.

But why?

Farah was drawing nearer to her first orgasm when he kissed her chin, pressed down on her lower back and exploded into her pussy. They came at the same time and gazed into each other's eyes.

He was a magician and his fuck game was like magic.

When his cell phone rang, with his dick still tucked inside her body, he carried her over to his bed and laid her down face up. Kissing her once before pulling out of her hotness. Glancing at his cell phone on the nightstand he turned toward her and sighed. "It's my wife, I have to answer this."

"No explanation needed, Rasim. I understand."

He lifted the handset and bopped into the bathroom as she observed his chiseled muscular physique. He was covered in so many tats that his skin was barely visible.

The man was moving art.

In the bathroom he flipped the light on and the door remained open. From her vantage point she could see him clearly. Pressing the phone against his ear he said, "Don't come over, Snow. I have company."

Silence.

"You wanted it this way so let it be," he continued.

Silence.

"Well I'm not fighting for us anymore either. It's over!" He ended the call and slammed the door leaving Farah confused.

The purpose of their meeting was blood and yet she hadn't quenched her thirst. Things had gotten so serious.

This was something she would have to remedy.

Advancing toward the bathroom she opened the door without permission. Startled, her jaw hung when she saw him tearing at a tattoo on his chest with the name Snow etched across his heart, a gate in front of it. The blade he was using was shoddy at best and didn't penetrate the skin deep enough.

Luckily for him she brought tools.

Embarrassed, he tossed the dull razor in the sink. "Why'd you come in here?" He frowned. "You're evading my privacy."

She moved in closer, his body language told her she was allowed. "Trouble in your relationship?"

"Trouble in my marriage," he corrected.

Farah eased in front of him so that her back was against the cool white sink. Removing the blade from her bra she smiled and looked up at him. The golden razor she was holding appeared to bling when it hit the light. "I can help you with that but first I have a question."

She was intriguing and he was all in. "I'm listening."

"Can I make you famous?"

He kissed her soft lips. "Sexy, I'm already a star."

Pussy juiced up, and without asking, she made the first slice across the tattoo and licked the blood as it oozed out. The man didn't wince but his dick pulsated and he wondered why it felt so good. Since he hadn't stopped her she lanced him again, and again, until five slices covered the tattoo in criss cross fashion. Her tongue slurping his crimson fluid.

Under her spell, Rasim lifted her up and placed her on the edge of the sink. He pushed her legs apart and eased into her tight pussy. Once inside he felt the need to make things clear. Gazing down at her pretty face he said, "We fight hard but I will never leave my wife."

She smiled. "And I will never leave him." She kissed him allowing him to savor his own salty fluid from her tongue.

Covered in blood, he fucked her viciously in the bathroom. It was one of the best sexual experiences she'd ever had.

And for that she left him alive.

CHAPTER TWENTY-ONE

SHADOW

"We Gonna Do The Plan Or Not?"

The new apartment Shadow and Mia moved into was tucked into a small town in Baltimore County, ten miles away from the old digs Della discovered. They were careful wanting to ensure nobody was following so they didn't relocate until 3:00 am in the morning, during whore hours.

Within the pitch black of the apartment, with only the moon shining inside to offer light, Shadow approached Farah. "You got it right, sis? Because everything has to play perfectly if this is going to work."

"Why you keep asking me like I'm a child?" She whispered. "We went over it five times already. I'm clear on my part." She paused. "You act like you don't trust me or something."

He was about to respond until Mia

grabbed her hand. "Listen, there's a possibility this could go wrong and you could end up in the hands of the Bakers. If that happens I can assure you that it won't be without a fight. But it don't mean you won't get hurt. Do you understand?"

"At least I know this will all be over if they get me. So yes." Farah separated from Mia, trudged to the couch and flopped down, boxes of clothes and dishes sat at her feet because they hadn't unpacked. "I don't want nobody else getting hurt."

"We can't worry about nobody but us, Farah," Mia said grabbing her hand. "We're at the point where we can only access bullets and moves."

She sighed. "I wish I never killed..."

"I don't want to know the details of what you did," Mia interrupted. "Whether you killed Knox or not is not a concern for the Cottons. We're family and we're going to see this thing through."

"So we gonna do the plan or not?" Shadow

asked.

"Shadow, I will be there," Farah said. "If not this thing will go on forever."

Within the darkness Shadow gazed at Mia. "Then it's settled, we move tomorrow."

Farah picked up the duffle bag on the floor. "What's in there?" Mia asked.

"A little something that will help an old friend."

CHAPTER TWENTY-TWO

SLADE

"Nobody You Need To Be Concerned About."

Slade lie face up as he stared at the metal rods on the bunk above his head. His frame, too large for the mattress, caused his limbs to spill over the sides, making it difficult to capture a good night's rest. He was about to dose off for a much needed nap when the bars came sliding open, rattling loudly.

"Baker," the Correctional Officer yelled. "You have a visitor."

Slade sat up and rubbed his tired eyes. "Who is it?"

"Nigga, get the fuck up and see for yourself. I ain't your wife."

Slade moved slowly toward the C.O. until he was upon him. Words were not said but his intimidating height as he stood over the officer had the official feeling unsafe. Now he realized it wasn't smart to use so much word play before and as a result he feared for his life. Clearing his throat he said, "Can you turn around please?"

Oh now he wanted to be polite.

Slade eyed him a little closer before rotating, the handcuffs clamping over his large wrists. When he was done he was led out of the cell to see who was waiting.

He had cold blue eyes and a mustache that covered his top lip. Down south Slade would stay clear of a man with similar features and yet this character claimed to come in peace.

Slade situated his muscular body in the chair as he stared across the table at high-powered attorney Ben Richards, a man claiming to work for him. "Do you understand everything I've said, Mr. Baker? Because I'm happy to answer any questions you may have."

"Let me see your business card."

Mr. Richards slid it across the table and Slade examined it fully. "I assure you, I'm as good as it gets."

Slade eyed the white card with blue words from the attorney once more. "So what does what you said mean for me? Because I was told this case was open and shut and that I would be doing time."

"And who told you that?"

"The first public defender. The incompetent one I fired."

Mr. Richards smiled arrogantly and shook his head. "Exactly, Mr. Baker. The only thing Public Defenders care about is checking off cases on their lists. Every now and again you're blessed with a serious attorney but most of them just want the job done." He exhaled. "I've even heard of PD's and

Prosecuting attorney's working together to seal a defendant's fate. Luckily for you none of that matters because you have me in your corner."

Slade looked at the card again as if he could read the lawyer's past. "So who hired you?"

The attorney sat back in his seat. "A beautiful woman...her name is Farah Cotton. She asked me not to tell you but if you're my client I feel you have the right to know."

"How could she afford you?"

"Not my problem. She entered my law office with a bunch of one hundred dollar bills and I handed her a receipt. I let her know I would be visiting you the same day and here I am." He entered a code to his dark chocolate briefcase and it flew open, revealing its contents. "Who is she anyway?"

Slade considered the question, trying to suppress the gratitude he had for her in that moment. She was his sworn enemy and it was important that he remember, no matter what she did for him in the instant. "She's nobody you need to be concerned about."

"Well that nobody paid a lot of money to see this thing through. Although after reviewing your case I feel bad." He removed a manila folder from his briefcase marked with *Baker* in a black Sharpie. "Had I known it would've been so easy I might not have charged her so much."

"Why you say that?" He frowned.

"You're here because the prosecution obtained a video in Platinum Lofts of you engaged in a fight with a Warren Farmer. In the beginning the tape looks consistent but the rest is pieced together." He chuckled. "Better than a Hollywood movie. Timeframes don't match and the whole thing appears doctored. With my skills there's no reason I shouldn't be able to get you out before your trial next month."

Slade's eyes widened. "So I can be...I can be..."

"A free man."

Slade was excited but buckled down as skepticism covered his hopes. "How do I know I can trust you?"

"Whether you do or not is up to you. The bill has already been paid. You just sit tight and stay out of trouble." He pointed at him. "We don't need you giving them a reason to keep you."

Now Slade was nervous and figured he might as well come clean. "I already...I mean there was this one incident."

"I'm aware of it." He waved his hand. "But make sure it's your last infraction or I'm out. Bill paid or not."

Later that day Slade walked into the visiting hall again only to see Farah. He shook his head and picked up the phone, doing his best not to look into her beautiful eyes. "What you doing here?"

"I wanted to see you, Slade." She paused. "Nothing more and nothing less."

"Well you shouldn't be here." He looked at her and then away again. Damn she was beautiful. Since he'd been in prison she'd done more for him than anyone and he hated and loved her for it. "Thanks for the lawyer though. I appreciate it."

She grinned. "No need to thank me."

"I have to. Unlike the situation with my brother, I'm in here on my own accord and you didn't have to help a nigga but you did."

She smiled. "It's because I love you, Slade. I told you that already."

"Stop it, Farah."

"I miss you."

"Stop fucking around or I'm walking out of the visit," he promised.

"Well how about this, I miss your fat dick, baby," She whispered causing him to stiffen instantly. "And how you felt deep inside my warm pussy."

It had been so long since he had that type of attention, especially from someone he adored and taught how to fuck. Her sexual talk combined with the hate he felt drove him insane. His dick was pulsating and he rested his hand in his lap as she continued to speak dirty. Before he knew it he came inside his pants, his nut against his skin.

"That's fucked up," he said angrily looking around to see who was watching. "Now I gotta go back with a stain on my pants and shit."

She giggled. "It's good to know I can still bring out the best in you."

He shook his head. "You think I'm a soft nigga and that's a mistake." He frowned. "When I get out of here I'm—"

She grew serious. "Today I'm going to see your family, Slade. It's over. All of it."

Slade's eyes widened. "What you talking about?"

"I'm going to give them the justice they wanted so this will be the last time I see you. *Ever.* I paid for you to have an attorney not to get back with you but so that you can be with your family after they kill me."

"Farah, don't do that shit. Let me—"

"It's done already, Slade and I'm sorry for everything I did to you. I'm sorry for hurting you. And I'm sorry for coming into your life." She placed her hand against the glass and put the phone on the table.

"Farah!" he screamed into it. "Farah, stop!

It was too late.

She was gone.

Farah exited the prison with tears running down her cheek. She was about to get into her rental when she was snatched by Bones and pulled to his car.

Farah's wrists throbbed because the blood circulation had been cut off from the ropes tied on her arms. Bones had her restrained in the basement next to an old water heater and she was beyond uncomfortable. Not only had he struck her several times, but he fed her heroin on the regular causing her thoughts to alternate from hate to lust respectively.

The feeling was bewitching.

She wanted it to stop so that she could think clearly and yet the drug made things easier to cope with.

After he shot her up with another dose he plopped in the chair in front of her. Even while high she was beautiful. "Why do you insist on breaking my heart, Farah? Huh? What did I ever do to you but help?"

"Bones, please, my brother, I have to, I have to meet him," she said nodding off. "I'm...I'm begging you not too—"

"Fuck your brother!" he yelled. "Do you hear me? Fuck him! That nigga lied on my name to get at them Bakers and it got back to me."

Her eyes widened because she didn't think he was aware Shadow used his name. Why would he be? As far as she knew he didn't have access to the Baker family. "How did you...?"

"Know?" He finished her sentence. "Let's just say Zashay ran into Willie again and he told me all about the upcoming plan. That nigga lied on my name, Farah. What should a man with as much power as me do about that?"

"Bones, I'm...I'm..." Slob hung along the sides of her mouth and she could no longer talk.

He exhaled and wiped it away with his dry thumb. "You're mine, Farah Cotton. In all of your evilness. And I'm going to keep pumping you with this good shit until you realize it." He swung a cellophane bag filled with dark cream dope and grinned.

CHAPTER TWENTY-THREE
SHADOW
"Let's Roll."

Shadow paced in circles in the living room of his apartment with his hands folded over his chest. "I knew she was gonna do this shit, Mia," He yelled. "You were telling me I was doing too much and look what happened. Everything is in line and we coming up short because she's not here. I should—"

"She's probably still coming, Shadow." She sighed looking out the window. "Let's give it a few minutes before you forge opinions."

"Why do you keep taking up for her? Look what time it is." He showed her the screen of his cell phone and stuffed it back in his pocket before she could even see it. "If she was coming she would've been here by now. I saw in her eyes she wasn't ready for this and I was right. Fuck!"

"What if something's wrong, Shadow? You out here blaming her and thinking the worse but what if something happened to your sister?"

He waved her off. "Nothing happened to that bitch. Not with that nigga following her everywhere she goes. She just let us down once again."

"I want to tell you something and you probably won't believe me." She paused. "But Farah wasn't afraid. I have a feeling she was going to give herself up for real. Without the plan."

"How you figure?"

"I saw it in her eyes. I think she was going to do it to save us and for Slade."

Shadow waved her off. He was not a believer. "Well we'll never get to find out now will we?" When his cell rang he pulled it out of his pocket and answered. "Hello..." He paused. "Okay, we're on our way out now." He stuffed it back into his pocket. "They're outside. Let's roll."

Shadow and Mia rushed outside where six of their cousins on their mother's side jumped out of a red pickup truck. All of them had deep dark chocolate skin without flaws, just like them. Shadow and Mia hadn't seen this side of the family since they were kids and it was Ashur, their father, who placed the call to bring them together. As children he isolated his family so much that they lost contact with their cousins so this was his way of making amends.

Considering the drama it could not have come at a better time.

Shadow and Mia hugged their family members and then Juicy, the oldest handed Shadow the phone. "It's your father. He wants to rap to you right quick."

While Shadow was on the phone Mia chopped it up with her family. "Hey, Dad, how you holding up?" He leaned against the truck.

"I'll be better if things work out today," he said. "But I got the books and money you and Mia sent so thank you."

"You don't have to thank us. It's what we do."

"Son, what's happening with Farah?" He sighed. "Why did you need so many of your cousins?"

Shadow looked down at the concrete and kicked an empty soda can. "Nothing you should worry about, pops."

"Son, I asked a question."

He rolled his eyes and sighed. "Dad, you know I can't talk on the phone even if I wanted to. Let's just say I'm doing all I can to handle a situation that's been brewing for a year. Like you would've done if you were home. You gotta leave it at that."

Ashur chuckled. "I keep forgetting you a man now." He paused. "I just worry so much in here because I can't help or protect you." He sighed. "Listen, how are you guys holding up with Elise being gone?"

"The best we can. I'm not gonna lie her murder keeps fucking me up and I won't rest anytime soon." Shadow focused on his cousins who were all smiles and laughing it up with Mia. If a person drove by they would not be able to tell they were preparing for war. "With time things will be good I guess."

"Okay, I'm gonna let you go but let me say this. Take care of each other, Shadow. Remember that at the end of the day if you don't have family you don't have shit."

"I hear you loud and clear, chief."

After he ended the call he handed Juicy back her phone. "So what now?" She asked. "And where's Farah?" She looked around. "I thought she was in on this plan."

"She couldn't make it", he said disappointedly. "But I got another idea."

CHAPTER TWENTY-FOUR

CUTIE

PRESENT DAY

Cutie slammed the diary closed, sat back and exhaled. She realized that after she finished a few more sections she would be done and she didn't want the narrative to end. Instead of completing the story right away, she opened the box and looked at the newspaper clippings inside. Running her fingers over the paper she relished the smoothness.

Everything about Farah and The Fold captivated her.

After reading all of the clippings she opened another blue book that was full of addresses. Her finger rolled down the pages until she found an entry that read *Mama's house*. Her eyes lit up as she realized this could possibly be where Mooney lived. Cutie recalled Mooney saying how she inherited the house despite living in the projects.

Could this be true?

Or was it all a lie?

Missing her friend again, Cutie stumbled over to the window and opened the blinds. She was inspired to visit the house but it was raining. "Mooney, can you help me? Please." She said to herself.

It wasn't long before it dawned on her that even if she wanted to visit she didn't have a dime to her name. And once there how would she get inside? There were no keys in the box and her plan sounded daunting.

Cutie decided not to think about it at home because it was time to move so she got dressed. She wanted to be brave like Farah, her hero. Once ready she slid on her jacket, grabbed Mooney's address book, the journal and opened her bedroom door.

Moving toward the exit she turned momentarily to be sure her foster mother wasn't coming. Surprisingly they weren't in the living room so she figured it was the best time to leave.

Opening the front door, she rushed outside and stumbled down the steps. The rain wasn't as powerful as it had been but it was still serious. Water washed off the sidewalks and into the streets causing some cars to hydroplane.

And yet at the moment nothing was more important than seeing Mooney's house and being close to her presence. With the diary, the address book and newspaper clippings clutched against her body she was about to hitchhike when a familiar truck pulled alongside her.

It was the man her foster mother was fucking earlier that day.

He rolled down the window to his Ford Explorer. "Where you going, girl?"

Cutie pretended she didn't hear him but the man was relentless. Recalling the weird way he gazed at her in the living room made her feel unsafe.

"I asked a question. Don't make me ask again." He maneuvered the car as his head stuck out of the window while yelling at her. "Where you going?"

Cutie stopped and noticed that suddenly rain was pouring down harder. At this rate she would be too wet to do anything but go home. "Going to see my other family.

"Your mama know that?"

"Yes."

"What's the address?" She rattled it off and he said, "Well get inside. I'll take you there."

Cutie sat in the passenger seat looking at the stranger every so often. Figuring it would be best to be nice she whispered, "Thank you, sir. For taking me and all."

"Yeah, well, you shouldn't be out here alone. It's too dangerous for a little girl." He scratched his balls and placed his hand on the steering wheel. "Not to mention night will be falling soon."

"Well thanks again, sir," she said under her breath.

He frowned. "Who live at this address anyway?"

"My auntie," she lied as he drove with one hand on the steering wheel why the other texted. "I haven't seen her in awhile and miss her that's all."

"Well you're lucky I came when I did."

Not feeling like talking she opened the diary and immersed herself into the pages. And just like that she was pulled back into Farah's world.

CHAPTER TWENTY-FIVE

AUDIO

"Answer The Phone."

Audio sped down the highway on the way to Platinum Lofts to inform his family about the news he uncovered. He knew where The Fold rested their heads and it was time to attack. The lead was crucial.

He would've gotten to his family earlier but disposing a body was not as easy as it appeared on television. First he had to find a quiet place for Tomi, which led him to one of the few heavily wooded areas in Maryland.

Using the cover of night, it took hours to properly conceal her body within the soft dirt. By the time he was done his cell phone battery was dead and he couldn't make the call to alert his family.

Once Audio arrived at the building he dapped Cheyenne and Yo who guarded the front door. "Damn, man, what happened to your clothes?" Cheyenne asked him. Cheyenne lifted his cap and scratched his scalp; his brown skin was potted and scarred.

Audio glanced down at his soiled jeans and t-shirt. "It's a long story. My fam upstairs?" He pointed at the door.

"Nope, they bounced earlier."

"Fuck," Audio said looking around. "You sure?"

"Positive," Yo interjected. He was a big man with bulging eyes and a serious weed habit. "They left about fifteen minutes ago so you just missed them." He glanced at his watch.

"Aight, thanks man." He dapped them both and dodged up the steps, avoiding the elevators all together.

When he arrived inside the apartment he was bummed to learn that they were correct. His family left the building. Based on the time he figured he had about an hour before the meeting with the Cottons. Rushing, he showered, jumped into clean gear and headed out. Before leaving he charged his phone and had just enough power to reach out to his brothers.

The first unanswered call went to Major and the second to Killa. When he prepared to call Grant he realized he didn't know his number by heart. Since they'd been family he never called him personally because Della and Killa always did. So he decided to worry about that later and hit it to the scene.

After purchasing a car charger he was on the highway and things were tense. Nervousness made it difficult for him to think straight and he needed help. "Knox, if you up there, man, don't let nothing happen to the fam. Please. I want to put this to an end."

On the road, he dodged in and out of traffic until he was struck with a moment of clarity. For some reason he recalled every digit of Grant's phone number.

Why did he recall it so clearly?

Whether it was Knox or not he appreciated the extra help.

With the information, he pulled the cell phone off the charger and dialed Grant's number. It rang a little longer than Killa's but still no answer. He thought all was lost until he looked ahead and saw the large grey RV Grant owned driving up the street. Tossing the phone down he pressed the gas pedal as hard as he could to catch up with him.

"If you not gonna slow down answer the phone, Grant! Fuck!" He punched the steering wheel.

CHAPTER TWENTY-SIX

KILLA

"I Told You A Million Times."

Grant drove his RV briskly up the highway, headed toward the destination to snatch Farah. At one point he was level headed about the Cotton ordeal but after Killa murdered his brother all he wanted was to bury the broad, grieve Judge's death and murder Audio in secret.

"When we get down there I'll do most of the talking," Grant said to Killa who was in the passenger seat. Major sat behind him in the back. "I don't want them moving before we have a chance to make the call, close in and snatch the bitch."

"You acting like we stupid niggas," Major said. "We went over the details a million times. As long as your people do what need be done on their end we good on the rest. Believe that."

Grant shook his head. "When did it become my people? We all blood related remember?"

"I ain't gonna lie, after the shit with Killa you haven't been moving right," Major said. "Energy not matching. Making me think after this Cotton shit you cutting us off."

"So now you talking for your brother, Major?" He looked over at Killa. "He's sitting right here and he's a grown man. Let him speak for himself."

"I made a mistake, fam," Killa said. "Told you a million times but you not hearing me."

Grant's cell phone rang and he welcome the distraction. Exposing his anger may have alerted them that he had ominous plans for Audio. Although the cell was in his lap he secretly kept it on silent. It was an attempt to avoid Audio who he was concerned wanted in on the operation. But the last thing he needed was his hotheaded behavior ruining shit. Fortunately for him this caller was important. "What's up?" Grant said into the phone.

"We're here and we have our sights on the girl," Tanoyka said. "What you want us to do?"

"Nothing," Grant responded excitedly. "We're going through with the plan to shut the park down. But keep eyes on them at all times." He paused. "How does the girl look? Is it Farah?"

"That's just it, they haven't said she's Farah or not. When we yelled across the park and asked if she was coming they wanted to know where you all were. Said she won't walk over here until you promise personally to end the war if she gives herself up."

He nodded. "What's the scene like?"

"About four niggas in red and black and the girl wearing a red hood who I think is Farah." She paused. "But I'm going to be honest. Something doesn't feel right."

"We'll be fine," Grant persisted. "Trust me. We gonna light that park up."

He hung up and placed the cell on his lap. "They there," he told his cousins. "Shit working out smoothly...just like I—"

When Killa noticed Grant's phone ringing again he said, "Audio hitting you up. Answer that shit."

Grant turned the phone off. "Nah, man. Can't do that."

Killa frowned. "Fuck you mean you can't do that?" He paused. "I been waiting on his call all day. The little nigga been out all night and I want to make sure he's aight."

"I'm gonna be honest with ya'll, Audio is a liability these days. Now I promised your mother I would leave him out of future matters and that's exactly what I'm gonna do. Don't forget, it was Aunt Della who called me out here so her word is solid."

"But we all paying you," Major added.

"Not to mention something may be wrong," Killa persisted. "What if he has some information for us?"

"Everything is wrong," Grant corrected

him. "Especially when it comes to that kid. Now I'm moving—" Grant's eyes widened as he looked in his rearview mirror.

"What now?" Killa asked, sensing his fear. He turned around to see for himself but the RV didn't have windows in his line of vision.

"It's your brother." Grant gripped the steering wheel. "He's following us."

"That's exactly what we're talking about," Major added. "Audio wouldn't be doing all this unless something is up. Call him back to see what he knows."

Before he could place the call two vehicles pulled alongside the RV. The car closest to the driver's side was filled with women with espresso colored skin. One of them waved at Grant and played with what looked like a large two-handed remote control, all with a smile on her face. "What's up with this bitch?" Grant said out loud.

Killa extended his head to see over Grant but he couldn't get a good look. "I don't know, but I'm getting bad vibes. Maybe you should pass them."

"Where the fuck I'm gonna go?" He pointed ahead. "I got cars in front and on every side." Suddenly Grant didn't think things were going as planned after all.

"Well something ain't right," Major said removing his two nine millis that were already loaded. "The next time you can get out of the way do it."

Grant continued to advance up the road when suddenly he heard a small thud on top of the RV. "What the fuck was—"

His question was halted when a small explosion blew off the roof of the vehicle. The woman holding the remote controller was operating a quad copter with a bomb attached. Grant lost control and careened to the right and slammed into a ditch, barely missing two cars.

Once the RV crashed eight women withdrew from the surrounding vehicles and fired into Grant's ride simultaneously. The

RV was too large for the women to know what progress was being made, in terms of bloodshed, so the plan was to load and reload until they were bullet free.

Commuters driving alongside the road made phone calls to the police but the women didn't care. The mission was accepted and they wanted the Bakers out of DC whether by plane, bus, car or body bag.

They were about to reload when suddenly one of the female shooters was struck from behind. "I been hit!" She yelled holding her arm, blood oozing everywhere.

They were trying to see where the fire was coming from but couldn't identify the gunman. "Get in the car, I'm gonna follow!" One of the ladies yelled.

The injured woman limped toward the vehicle.

The others were going to continue to bust until another one received a bullet to the thigh. "Who the fuck is that?" she screamed.

If the scene weren't so anxious they would've spotted Audio ducking behind cars for cover. Instead they piled into their rides and tried to get away while Audio, no longer hiding, fired at them in plain view. It took a lot of gas power and scraping alongside of other cars but eventually they were able to escape from the chaotic scene.

Leaving Audio alone.

CHAPTER TWENTY-SEVEN

FARAH

"You Hurt Me More."

Farah was tied to a chair with Bones standing in front of her. The expression on his face alternated from anger to depression as he grappled with why the women in his life never appreciated him. "You lied to me this entire time, Farah."

"I never lied to you," she cried. "But what you're doing now is wrong. How can you expect me to love you if you're treating me this way? Look at me! You got me tied up like a dog and yet you claim to love me."

"Did you steal from me, Farah? Did you take my money out of this house?"

Farah moved around uneasily. "I don't know what you mean."

"Did you take my fucking money or not?" He yelled.

She was about to lie when she was struck

over the top of the head. The pressure was excruciating and suddenly she felt nauseous. Before he hit her she didn't know he had a weapon. Had she known she would've considered her response a little more seriously. But it was too late and as a result she was struck with a horsewhip, blood pouring from her scalp.

"DID YOU TAKE MY FUCKING MONEY?"

Warm tears rolled down her cheeks and soothed the fresh cut on her skin. "Yes, I did and I'm sorry, Bones."

He plopped into his chair and wiped the sweat from his brow. "Why, Farah?"

She looked up at him. "To get him out of jail."

He raised his eyebrows and tilted his head. "So you spent my dough, to get another nigga out of prison? Knowing that the last person I wanted free was him?"

"If I give you an answer you'll hit me. If I don't you'll hit me too. So do whatever you want. I don't care anymore."

He peered into her eyes, took a deep breath and stood up. It was time to hang her a little. Walking behind her he untied the ropes holding her arms. Once free she struck him as hard as she could in the face and made a run for the steps. Being tied for hours she was weak and he was able to catch her, yanking her to the floor by the back of her hair.

For trying to escape he hammered her with body blows until he was tired.

It was midnight when Zashay crept down the steps. She'd been following Bones all day, hiding in the corners of the mansion to see what he was up to. Wanting to know what was going on in the basement she eventually sucked his dick until he fell into a coma like sleep. It always did the trick and only then did she retreat down the stairs.

Flipping the light on she was shocked to find Farah tied up on a chair alone. Her face was bloodied and bruised and she was unrecognizable. She covered her mouth in shock. Zashay knew he could be violent but never with this kind of abuse.

"Why would he do this?" Zashay said to herself. "You should've gotten away when you could."

Farah opened her left eye and gazed up at her. When her neck felt heavy she dropped her head and remained silent.

"I know you hate me, Farah and I despised you too but things are different now." She paused. "I finally under—"

"You hurt me more than he did, Zashay. You hurt me because I was starting to care about you. But now I know everything you said to me was a lie."

"It's not that way. I thought he loved me and—"

"Fuck you, Z!" She paused. "Just go upstairs and leave me to die! I don't want to hear anything you have to say."

Zashay wiped away the creeping tears from her face. Did she love her more than she realized? "I'm going to let you go."

Farah sat up straight, pain ripping through every area of her body. "What about Bones? He'll kill you."

She crossed her arms over her body and rubbed briskly. "Fuck Bones," She smiled half-heartedly. "Right?"

Shadow was infuriated as he examined Farah's face. Part of him wanted to snatch another Baker off the street but the other part hated himself for accusing Farah of letting him down. Before she was assaulted Mia posed the question of what if something was wrong and he disregarded her statement, only to learn big sis was right.

To make matters worse she was claiming that a 'stranger' was responsible when Shadow believed in his heart it was a Baker. He never suspected Bones for an instant.

"I'm sick of this shit," Shadow yelled. "I should go blow Platinum Lofts up right now!"

Mia, who was crying and hysterical, was too beside herself to speak on the issue. Farah was virtually unrecognizable and it ripped at her heart.

"Shadow, I said they weren't involved." She pointed at her face. "And this looks worse than it feels. But I need all of this to stop because I can't take it anymore." She exhaled. "And I'm here to tell you to let it go."

"Farah, we shot up the Baker RV." He paused. "Me and our cousins while you were away. So if you—"

Farah grabbed his hand. "What...what you mean shot up the Baker RV?" He remained silent. "Shadow, what are you saying?"

"Just what you heard."

Her eyes widened and she prayed to God whoever got hurt was anybody outside of Audio, Major or Killa. Slade couldn't take another sibling loss. "Who was in it?"

"I don't know but we got them mothafuckas for sure. Juicy and the girls unleashed on that bitch."

"But what happened with the meet up?" She paused. "How did that go down?"

"When you didn't show we pulled a bitch off the street to play the part and pretend she was you. So it worked out fine I guess. They fell for the trap."

"So what was the plan?"

"The plan was to make the Bakers think we were at the secret location. Which we were with a girl wearing a hoodie with your complexion. Most of her face was hidden but from the distance I know they couldn't be sure," he continued excitedly. "Anyway when Juicy and them opened fire on the RV and we got word we fired at the men in the park. They busted back but nobody got hit. Niggas just fled the scene."

"Oh, Shadow." She placed her hand on her forehead. "This is so bad."

"Farah, they had a plan for us too. I'm telling you they were going to kill us all. We were just smarter because we knew the road they had to come down to meet us at the park. And instead of waiting we brought court to the highway. That's the only reason we still alive."

Farah looked at him and backed up into the wall. Her gaze fell from her brother and her temples throbbed. She could feel hives rising on her skin and suddenly she felt faint. All of her life she'd been selfish and allowed what she wanted to lead her actions. But now her family was dropping like flies and it had to stop.

The thing was this...she loved the Bakers too. Just couldn't admit it out loud.

Yes the Bakers had bloodshed coming. And yes they killed her grandmother but had she surrendered no one else would've gotten hurt. Farah ran her hands down her face, took a deep breath and walked up to him. "I can't do this anymore." She moved toward the door. "I'm sorry."

"What are you going to do?"

"What I should've done a long time ago."

Farah sat in Shadow's car with her cell phone pressed against her ear. She wasn't sure if she was going to reach anyone in the apartment but she hoped Slade's number was the same and that more than anything his brothers were still alive.

After three rings the call was answered. "Hello," someone said groggily.

She swallowed, having recognized his voice. "Killa, it's me." She whispered. "Farah. Now I know you won't believe me but I'm ready to meet you anywhere you want. You pick the location. I don't care anymore. I just need this all to stop."

CHAPTER TWENTY-EIGHT

KILLA

"Fuck!"

The wind was ferocious as Killa stood outside next to his car, a busy highway between him and a patch of land on the other side. After the war with the Cottons he suffered a bullet wound to the upper arm, which was far better than Grant's fate. Two bullets to the head and he was quickly sent to the afterlife with his brother Judge and the family in Mississippi was ready for war. It took a lot of pleading to get them to stay put. The worst part was he wasn't all that upset about Grant's death.

After Judge died he didn't trust him.

Major was also struck in the thigh and was at home resting with Audio looking after him. Things seemed to be calm in the streets but they couldn't be sure which was why they were leaving Platinum Lofts later that week.

He figured once he got his hands on Farah he could put the war behind him.

When he saw a car park across the street, where Farah told him she'd be, he stood up straight. Within seconds Farah eased out and stood along the highway. His hand hovered over the weapon on his hip and he examined the passing cars prepared to fire if he detected a set up.

"What happened to her face?" he said to himself.

Audio begged him not to go but something in Farah's voice told him she was as fed up with the bloodshed as he was, so he went with his gut without telling Audio a word.

Tears rolled down Farah's cheek, as she looked left and right preparing for the break in traffic. The moment she spotted her chance she stepped into the street until a car sped in front of her and snatched her inside.

"Fuck!" Killa screamed as he anticipated bringing the war to an end. He tucked the gun into his waist and held the sides of his head as the car sped down the road. He'd come so close and now all he could do was watch the SUV pull off with his prize.

Annoyed, Killa jumped into his car and hit the steering wheel several times in anger. He was tired of this shit and was growing frustrated as the days passed. Just like Judge he was another person with a secret. Some time back he met a beautiful woman in DC and had gotten her pregnant. Now his intentions were to stay in the city he hated, knowing his mother would never approve.

He hadn't told a soul, not even his brothers.

When his phone rang he removed it from his pocket and took a deep breath when he saw Audio's number. "Is Major okay?" Killa asked answering the phone.

"He's resting but I got better news."

"What is it, man?"

"It's Slade. He getting out some time today!"

CHAPTER TWENTY-NINE

FARAH

"You Have Me And I'm Not Going Anywhere."

Farah sat in the back of a small van with Bones' weighted arm draped around her back. There were two rows of seats facing each other and Slade sat across from them, anger painted on his face. She wanted nothing more than to hug him but knew that would mean blood— not the drinking kind.

Bones other hand held a gun aimed at him as Farah's heart rocked because she knew that this was the moment she and Slade would die together.

Trailing the van was Mayoni, Carlton and Zashay in another vehicle.

"So this is the nigga you spent my money on huh? This is the nigga you can't live without?" Bones said as he looked at Farah before his gaze fell back on Slade. In his opinion he was ordinary. "That black mothafucka over there."

"Bones—"

"Answer me, bitch!" He screamed causing Slade to move forward before Bones cocked his gun. "Sit the fuck back down." When he kept moving toward him, Bones pointed at Farah's head freezing Slade's movements instantly. Bones laughed. "I knew that would get your attention."

"What the fuck you want with me, nigga?" Slade roared. "Huh? Because you know if you didn't have that gun you'd be dead by now." His hands crawled into fists that he clutched on top of his knees.

"I'm not scared of you. Even if I put this gun down it wouldn't help you one bit, partna. I stay nice with the hands."

Slade laughed. "How about you talk less and prove more."

Farah turned toward Bones. "Please let him go. You have me and I'm not going anywhere. I'm begging you not to do this. You were right about me. I was selfish and I won't be that way anymore if you give me a chance. I want to be better and I don't care about him."

Her words counteracted her conduct. She was crying so hard she was hysterical which angered him even more. Seeing how much she cared for another man had him swimming with fury.

"Is that why your brother called and said you were meeting Killa? Because you don't give a fuck about him?" His jaw twitched. "You were gonna let that dude kill you just to keep this punk over here alive. Stop playing games, Farah. I'm hip to your shit now." He chuckled. "What I don't get is why you didn't tell Shadow what I did to you. Had you done it he would've never called me." He looked at Slade and winked. "What you think, man? You like my fist work?"

Slade's muscles buckled and begged him with his eyes to stay where he was.

Farah noticed that Slade's facial

expression changed dramatically upon hearing that she was prepared to offer her life for his. Emotions were swirling but what was clear was that he loved her unconditionally.

"Bones, he doesn't mean anything to me, I promise," she lied. Placing her hand on his face she said, "All I care about is you. Let him go so that we can go about our life."

Slade moved uneasily in his seat. Had Bones not possessed the gun he would've been dead by now but everything had to be done in time. "Is that right?" Bones smirked. "You love a nigga that much, huh?"

"Yes, baby." She smiled, body trembling. "It's true and I'm going to prove it to you."

"Then look over there and tell him you don't love him anymore."

"Bones, I—"

"LOOK OVER THERE AND TELL THAT BLACK NIGGA!" He pointed at him.

Farah's gaze slowly moved toward Slade and her stomach bubbled. It was difficult to stare at him. Not only because she felt guilty but also because what she was about to say was untrue. But when she tried to fix her lips to lie, the words wouldn't exit.

There was no use.

They were going to die anyway.

Might as well tell the truth.

"I love you, Slade," she said truthfully. "I'm so sorry for all of the problems I caused."

Slade looked into her eyes. "And I love you too. More than you will ever know."

Enraged Bones removed his arm from around her neck and brought the butt of the gun alongside her face.

A cool stream of water poured down Farah's face and awakened her roughly. She moaned a little until Bones grabbed a grip of her hair and positioned her gaze so that she could see directly out of the window. "Wake up, beautiful," Bones whispered in her ear. "Because I want you to see this shit."

When Farah opened her eyes she saw Carlton and Mayoni across the way at a park. Mayoni held a gun aimed at Slade, looked at the van and fired twice at his abdomen causing Slade to drop to the ground.

She fainted.

Farah lie face down on the bed in a mansion sobbing uncontrollably. Thoughts of when she first met Slade rushed to her mind and she missed him already. He was the love of her life and she would never get to see what they could've been together. To make matters worse Bones had dug his claws in her so deeply that to refuse him meant her brother and sister would also die.

What could she do but live in misery?

Flashes of when she first met Slade came to mind. She was about to get assaulted by Kirk, her next-door neighbor in Platinum Lofts, when Slade with his 6-foot 5-inch frame bopped into the hallway. His presence was huge and she felt comforted when he entered instantly. His dark skin, his baldhead and even the scar that ran across the right side of his neck made him appealing.

Farah never, in her entire life, wanted a man more than she did him. And now he was gone forever.

When she heard the door unlock she sat up in bed, afraid Bones was entering to rape her again. Instead it was Mayoni. "How you holding up?"

She frowned and rolled her eyes. "You killed the one man in the world I would've given my life for and you ask me that shit?" Her anger was bubbling at the surface and she thought about murder. "You tell me, how would you feel if I took Carlton's life? Because I'm plotting as we speak."

"Farah, you need to—"

"I need to what?" She yelled. "I spent months in this bitch being somebody I'm not. I pretended to be meek so that Bones would feel stronger. And look where it got me! I will never, ever, love Bones after what he did! *EVER*. And if he plans on keeping me in this mansion I will tell him daily how much I hate him just to break his fucking heart."

"You would do that even though it will kill him. Because there's nobody he wants more than you."

"*Especially* because he wants me."

Mayoni sighed. "Come with me, Farah. I have to show you something."

"Do I have a choice?" She sighed.

"No, but trust me."

Mayoni and Farah walked toward room 568 of a run down motel on the outskirts of Baltimore City. Before going inside Mayoni looked around to make sure no one was watching their moves. When the door opened Farah almost fainted when she saw Carlton inside, holding a gun aimed at Slade.

He was alive!

The love of her life was breathing.

Overcome with joy she rushed up to him and wrapped her arms around his neck before kissing him passionately. "But I saw you." She kissed him again. "You were shot." She looked at Mayoni. "What's going on? I'm confused."

Was she dreaming?

Only to be reawakened in a nightmare?

"He'll explain everything," Mayoni said nodding at Slade. "You have thirty minutes to enjoy each other and not a second more."

When the rules were laid down Carlton and Mayoni walked out. Slade squeezed her once more before separating. "Farah, I...I..."

He plopped down on the edge of the bed, his thoughts swimming. "I'm confused. What is all of this shit? Who are these people?"

"It's a long story and I don't want to spend every minute on the details." She sat next to him and placed her hand over his. "Slade, what happened in the park? I thought you were dead."

He exhaled. "The Asian chick said when she fired I had to drop. At first I was going to try and overpower her and take the gun but she and that dude with the chewed up nose begged me to go along with the plan. I figured she had the weapon so if she wanted me dead I'd be gone already. So I played the part." He paused. "The next thing I know the van pulled off and they brought me here."

"But did she say why?"

"Shit moved so quickly, Farah. She said something about if they killed me you would never be happy with that nigga. And that they needed you to play the role." He paused. "Farah, who are they?"

Farah rubbed her pulsating temples. "I made a mistake, Slade. I made a big one and there's no way out of it. At first I was gonna try and leave and take my chances anywhere in the world. But now you're alive and I still have Mia and Shadow to think about. If I don't act how they want me to they'll really kill you this time."

"Farah, I'm home now and I can protect you." He said seriously. "Nobody can harm me."

"Slade, it's not that easy." She paused. "If all we had in the world was each other things would be simple. But you have your brothers, your mother and your cousins. I have my siblings. Everybody can't run and if we did they would never be safe."

He grabbed her hand and she stood in front of him. He opened his mouth and closed it before taking a deep breath. "Every night I spent in that cell I envisioned killing you because of Knox."

"It was a mis—"

"Don't say anything, Farah. Just hear me out because I've never been in a situation like this." He sighed. "I wanted to kill you. Even now my mind tells me to squeeze the breath out of your body. But when I saw that nigga with his hands on you, and your face, I realized I...I couldn't..."

"Slade, I'm sorry," Farah said dropping to her knees. "I'm sorry for everything and will spend the rest of my life blaming myself. But we can't...we can't be together." She paused. "If we do they'll kill you and I will die if that happens. I almost did."

"Leave DC with me, Farah. Come with me."

"Even if I wanted to your family hates me. My family despises you and The Fold won't allow it. Don't you understand, this will forever be forbidden love and I want you to..." She choked up. "I want you to find someone who can take care of you and make you happy." Basketball sized tears crawled down her face. "I want her to treat you how you deserve to be loved."

He looked into her eyes because she was talking foolishly. "I will never, ever, love a woman the way I love you."

Slade lowered his head and pressed his lips against hers. Slowly she rose and removed his shirt. Leaning back on the bed she crawled on top of him, as they remained engulfed in a kiss. The only breaths they took were to remove their clothing.

Naked, Slade positioned her body so that he could gaze down at her flesh. Taking her exquisiteness in he ran his chocolate hand over her yellow skin, loving how their tones looked together. Her body trembled as he kissed her belly, sending her into an immediate calmness.

Her man was home.

"I'll never love him, Slade," she cried. "I'll always hold you in my heart even if they keep us apart."

Slade remained silent and eased his stiff dick into her waiting body. As he filled her up she bit down on her bottom lip, the chemistry they had between them awakening.

"Fuuccccck," Slade moaned. "I miss this pussy so much." He kissed the side of her face. "I love you so much, Farah. What you do to my heart? How did you get into my mind?"

Farah wrapped her arms around his body, her lips pressed against his shoulder. The more he pressed into her soft flesh the wetter she got, her cream spilling out onto the sheets.

When he felt her teeth he rose and gazed down at her for a moment. "Where is your blade?"

Her eyes widened. "What? What do you mean?"

"Your blade, where is it?" He paused. "Don't bother lying...Audio told me what you do."

"In...in my bra, on the floor." She pointed in the direction.

He eased out of her, grabbed her bra and handed her the blade that was in the pocket. "I want to be a part of whoever you are. And if blood is it I want you to let me in.

Before she could dispute Slade sliced into his shoulder and allowed the burgundy blood to trail out. Easing his dick back into her body he maneuvered his arm so that his blood drizzled on her mouth. Clawing at his back she sucked and sucked until her lips throbbed.

Slade was surprised at how much he was turned on.

At that moment she realized she loved him more. Not because he allowed her to feast but because he proved that no matter what he was willing to go the extra mile.

He finally accepted who she was.

A vampire.

And they continued to explore each other until Mayoni knocked on the door.

Ending their time together.

After she was dressed Farah returned to the car as Slade was driven away with Carlton. Her eyes remained on the vehicle until it was out of sight. "I would've given you more time, Farah. But Bones will be up soon and you have to be home. Zashay sucked his dick to make him pass out but he won't sleep forever."

"She know it was for me?"

"Yes, she's on your side."

She sighed. "How do I know Carlton won't kill Slade?"

"Because he'll be in contact with you on this," she handed her an old flip cell phone. "Put it in a safe place."

"Thank you," Farah said as she wiped her tears. Her face still throbbed from all of the bruises.

"They can never come back to DC. *Ever.* Tickets have already been purchased for Slade and his family and they have to get out of the city." She paused. "Do you hear what I'm saying? You can never see him again."

A tear rolled down her face. "All this for Bones?"

Mayoni sighed. "I know it's a lot but we need Bones in his right frame of mine, Farah. And he won't be if you're not happy. I don't know why you have this hold over him but you do. So this is the plan. You will fake like you love him. You will put a smile on your face when you return to the mansion and you will care for him. He must not detect anything is off. This is very important."

"And if I don't?"

"Then I'll send some vamps to Mississippi to kill everybody with the last name Baker.

And this time I'll come for Mia and Shadow too."

Farah ran her hand down her face. "What are you going to do about the Bakers killing Lootz?"

"We told Bones that Grant was responsible. And since Shadow successfully murdered him that debt is over."

"So this is my life forever? I'm a prisoner?"

Mayoni placed her hand on her thigh. "Don't look at it like that. Why are you so sad? You are a vamp, Farah. And we are vamps. Even if you were with Slade he will never understand fully what it means to feed." She paused. "We are your family now and you can never forget it. Please don't make me show you our power. I will if I have to."

Farah's head hung. "So what now?"

"Tonight I want to cheer you up with Shikar."

Farah's eyes widened. "We're going on a hunt?"

"You feel better already. Don't you?"

Blue lights illuminated the massive indoor pool as *Future's* voice lit up the airwaves from the internal booming speakers on the wall. The *All White Swim Party* was packed and everyone felt on top of the world, especially Monica and Renee. Wearing tiny white bikinis, their asses and titties spilled over the thin material causing all the niggas in the vicinity to take notice as they switched to their reserved space.

Tossing their designer beach bags on the lawn chairs, they plopped down and looked around at all of the men. "I can't believe this shit," Renee said, flinging her long black braids over her shoulder. "I mean free food and free liquor? What the fuck?"

Monica dug through her purse and pulled out her chapstick, smoothing it over her pink lips. "I told you some rich niggas throwing this shit." She shrugged. "What do we give a fuck if it's free or not? Bitch, we on one tonight."

"I hear you but what's the name of the people throwing it again?"

"I don't know," Monica said. "The girl at the blood clinic gave me the flier after we got our results today for that nursing job. The only name on it was *T and F Presents.*" She looked around. "Now that I think about it I saw that dude over there in the clinic too." She pointed at a cutie in a Baltimore Ravens cap.

"This is weird but I love it. Seems so exciting!"

Abruptly the music ceased and the double doors flung open. Everyone turned to see what was happening when suddenly twelve beautiful people strolled inside. Their movements were so controlled they appeared to float on air.

The men were dressed in expensive black slacks and red button down shirts while the women wore black dresses accented with a hint of red.

Peeling himself from the group, holding Farah's hand, Bones stepped in front of the pack with a smile. Addressing the party he said, "My name is Carter but my friends call me Bones. We thank you all for joining us on this night to remember."

He gazed at Farah and she turned toward the crowd. "Now tell me good people...can I make you famous?"

EPILOGUE

Cutie slammed the diary shut, upset that she finished the story. What was she to do with her life now? An emptiness sat in the pit of her stomach and made her ill because tomorrow when she arose there would be nothing to look forward too.

She could read the journals again but it wouldn't be the same.

Jones, the driver, pulled up in front of the address Cutie requested and parked. He looked at her and sighed. "You sure your aunt lives here?" He gazed at the place.

She exhaled and looked at the house. The rain stopped, which made it a little easier to see. "Yes, I'm sure."

"Well go 'head. I'm gonna wait so hurry up. Don't be in there all day."

Cutie quickly hopped out of the car and ran toward the front door. She knew Mooney wasn't there because she was dead but she wanted to be near her presence. When she made it to the black lacquer door she knocked a few times and a tall white woman opened it immediately. "Who are you young lady?" She frowned looking down at her. "And what are you doing at my house?"

Cutie pulled the diary and address book closer to her chest, as if for protection. "Ummm...did a lady name Mooney use to live here?"

"A lady name Mooney?" She placed her hands on her hips. "What on earth are you talking about?"

"She was supposed to live here at one point. Probably before you I think."

"And when was that exactly?"

"I don't know," she shrugged, "maybe when she was a kid or something."

"That's impossible because I have been living in this house since I was a child. You sure you have the right place?"

Cutie looked down at the address book in her hand and checked the location. Then she glanced at the number on the door. "It's the same."

"Well in that case its also wrong."

"But I don't understand...this was...this was her house. Mooney would never lie to me."

"Look, I don't know who you are but don't come around here again." She pointed her pale finger in her face. "Next time I'm calling the police." She slammed the door and Cutie ran to the car crying all the way.

When she made it to the vehicle she was surprised to see Melinda. She stood next to the passenger side window knowing she was about to dig into her shit. "How did you...I mean..."

"Jones texted me and told me where you were going. Denise from downstairs ran me to the store and he heard you leave the house. Figured you were running away since Mooney died so he went after you and texted me." She paused. "Now get in the car, Cutie," Melinda snapped and she obeyed, easing into the backseat. "What the fuck are you doing around here anyway? And who was that woman? An old foster mother?"

Tears rolled down Cutie's face. "No. I wanted to...I wanted to see Mooney's house. The one her mother left her before she died."

She frowned. "How she have a house like that when she lived in the projects? Does that make any sense to you?"

"Yes, she said she wanted to live there to be around me and stuff. But her real house was here." She pointed at the home.

Melinda looked at Jones and shook her head. Without asking for permission she grabbed the things Cutie carried out of the house and thumbed through the items. She observed one of the newspaper clippings and showed Jones.

"Put that back!" Cutie yelled. "That's Mooney's!"

"Cutie, what do you think this is?""

"A newspaper about Farah."

Melinda shook her head and slowly peeled off a picture of Farah with a fake headline taped to a real article that read, *Farah Cotton...woman or vampire.* "Look again, Cutie. What do you see now?"

Cutie tilted her head and squinted. Now she was observing a picture of a car accident in the place of the photo she believed was genuine. "But...I don't...understand. Why would Mooney do this to me? Why would she lie?"

Melinda exhaled. "She was mentally ill, Cutie. Had early stages of dementia and everybody knew it. Don't get me wrong, she was a nice lady, which is why I didn't mind you staying with her from time to time, but she was not well."

Cutie felt anger welling up inside of her. How dare Melinda's freak whore ass talk about her only friend so badly. "You a liar! Farah is real and she lives in a mansion with The Fold. You just don't want me to know the truth because you think I'm too young. But I'm not young and I know what's real."

Melinda grew increasingly frustrated and snatched the diary from the child. She flipped page after page in anger. "Look at this shit, Cutie. This ain't nothing but the makings of a whack ass book. If it's a diary from Farah's point of view how can she know what everybody's thinking? Slade, Audio, Bones? What is this shit? It doesn't make any sense!"

"I DON'T BELIEVE YOU!" Cutie screamed beating the sides of her head. "I HATE YOU! I HATE YOU!"

Melinda exhaled and took the address book next. She thumbed through it and said, "What happened when you knocked on the door, Cutie?" When she continued to scream Melinda slapped her, silencing her instantly. "I asked you a question. Now what happened when you knocked on the fucking door?"

"The lady said Mooney never lived there," she pouted holding her cheek.

"Exactly! Now what will it take for you to believe me? Because I care about you, Cutie. I really do. But you're making it hard for me to let you stay in my house."

Jones pulled off the main road and along a private tree lined street. They drove a mile away from the entrance before settling on a black iron wrought gate.

He parked and Melinda turned around and looked at the little girl. "Cutie, I don't know about this." She looked at the address in the phonebook and then the numbers on the gate. "This doesn't seem real."

"I don't care if it is or not," Jones interjected. "At this point I've been driving you both around for hours. A shot of pussy not gonna be nearly enough for this fare." He pointed at the floor.

"You talk that shit when we get back to the house," Melinda said grabbing at his crotch, calming him down instantly. "I bet you'll be singing a whole new tune then."

"Can you go to the intercom thing at the gate, ma?" Cutie asked with wide eyes. "Please?"

She tilted her head. "Oh now I'm ma?"

"I'm begging you." Cutie positioned her hands as if she were praying. "I gotta know. I just gotta."

Melinda shook her head and approached the intercom with Cutie following. Afraid, although she wasn't sure why, she pressed the button to connect. "Hello, the voice said from the speaker. "How can I help you?"

"Uh...is Farah Cotton there?" Cutie asked.

Silence.

Melinda looked down at Cutie with a knowing look. She was almost certain that just like the other house, nothing would amount of this visit. Still she wanted to put this vampire thing to rest so that they could go on with their lives.

"You have the wrong address," the voice said. "Get off the property."

Melinda grabbed her hand. "Now will you please leave this alone?"

She moved for the car but Cutie shook her off and went for the intercom. Pressing the button again she said, "Is Bones there?"

"Who is this?" The voice said more angrily. "And what are you still doing on the property?"

"My name is Cutie...and I'm a friend of Mooney."

A few seconds later the voice returned. "How do you know Mooney?"

Melinda and Cutie's eyes widened believing they were getting somewhere after all. "She was a friend of mine," Cutie said. "But she died a little while ago."

A few seconds passed and the gates rolled open. Feeling like it was an invitation, Cutie dipped inside before they closed with Melinda following with flaring arms. "Hold up, Cutie!" She called out. "I don't trust this place!"

She could run her mouth all she wanted the girl was already gone until she happened upon a double black lacquer door. It was so large it was intimidating and before long a handsome man with neat dreads running down his back exited with three women.

"What you say about Mooney?" He asked, his voice booming. He stood over the child in an intimidating manner.

"Are you...are you Bones?" Cutie questioned, her eyes glistening.

He looked back at the women before focusing on Melinda and Cutie again. "I asked what you say about Mooney?"

"Uh, she was murdered a few weeks ago. Her funeral was today and she's a friend of mine." She paused, sadness visiting her again. "Well, she *was* a friend of mine. Did you know her?"

"You mean outside of her trying to break in my house, forcing me to chop off her arm?"

Cutie stumbled. "You were the one who cut her?"

"Listen, I don't know what Mooney told you but you better forget everything she said. The woman was off her rocker anyway. Don't be spreading lies."

"No problem, we're out of here," Melinda said trying to snatch Cutie away from the volatile scene. "Come on, we have to go home."

"Get off of me!" Cutie yelled pulling away. "She wrote about you in her journal, Bones. I know almost everything there is to know about you."

Bones glared down at her and stepped closer. "Mooney wrote about me? In that book right there?" He pointed.

"Yes," Cutie said.

He snatched it away and flipped through the pages. It was obvious that the property now belonged to him. "But there's more," Melinda said, sensing they were in danger. "A whole series of them back at my house." She wanted him to know if he killed them the secret was still out.

Bones smiled sinisterly. "How convenient."

Suddenly the door opened wider and a light skin woman with a red chiffon flowing dress exited the premises. She looked regal and was the most beautiful woman Cutie had ever seen. "Did she write about me too, little girl?" the woman questioned.

"Are you Farah Cotton?" Cutie asked, as she felt herself on the verge of crying.

She nodded. "Yes...I am."

Cutie ran up to her and hugged her legs before separating. "Mooney spoke so much about you." She said excitedly. "You are the most interesting woman I know!"

"You shouldn't have come here," Farah said seriously. "You should never have come."

Cutie's heart rocked in her chest. "Are your friends The Fold? Are you vampires?"

Farah looked back at Bones and down at Cutie. Now she'd said too much to ever leave.

Although they didn't answer when Cutie glanced at their clothing and saw tiny T's and F's embedded in the fabric she had her answer.

And it was all the confirmation she needed.

CHARACTER KEY

THE COTTONS

Farah Cotton

Farah hated her lighter skin when she was younger due to every member in her family being dark. As she got older she became arrogant about her complexion believing it gave her privileges. With time her perspective changed. Born with Porphyria, which causes blemishes when she's stressed she drinks blood to ease her pain. We later learned that Ashur, the man she thought was her father was not. Instead it was Jay, her Physical Education teacher in high school.

Shadow Cotton

Shadow is Farah's brother.

Mia Cotton

Mia is Farah's older sister. Had issues with her weight and is a master plan creator.

Chloe Cotton

Chloe is Farah's youngest sister who died in a car accident in which her boyfriend, Audio Baker was also present. We learned it was because Theo Cunningham, the boy the Cottons tormented in the beginning of Redbone, ran her off the road. Chloe later died.

Brownie Cotton

Brownie was Farah's mother. Throughout Farah's life Brownie tormented her because of her lighter skin. Brownie was later murdered by Theo but finished off by Farah.

Ashur Cotton

Ashur, a closeted homosexual, is Mia, Shadow and Chloe's birth father. For years Farah thought he was her birth father despite her light skin. Ashur went to prison for murdering a family in broad daylight at the bus stop.

Elise Gill

Elise Gill, who also suffers from porphyria, is Brownie's mother. She had Brownie at 12 years old. She doesn't wash because household products exacerbate her condition.

THE BAKER BOYS

Slade Baker

Slade is the love of Farah's life. He is very strong and the oldest of the brothers in his family.

Audio Baker

Audio is the youngest brother of the Bakers. He's hot headed and a loose cannon.

Major Baker

Major is also Slade's brother. He sold weed as a kid.

Brian 'Killa' Baker

Killa is Slade's brother. Gambles heavily and enjoys weapons. He learns to always examine the eyes to see the truth versus what they say.

Knox Baker

Knox is Slade's brother. He robbed houses as a kid and ran from Mississippi with the evidence necessary to keep his family out of prison. Farah killed him in her house.

Judge

Judge is the Baker Boys cousin. He killed a lot of people. He's 6 feet tall and ugly as a rhino. His brother is Grant.

Grant

Grant is the Baker Boys cousin He killed a lot of people. He's 5'5" tall, makes the decisions for his brother Judge. Grant wears a stiff smile at all times and he enjoys killing.

THE FOLD

Bones

Bones is second in charge of The Fold. Responsible for keeping things ticking. He's obsessed with Farah Cotton and was a former patient at Crescent Falls Mental Institution. Has long neat dreadlocks running down his back. Loves inflicting pain for sexual gratification

Mayoni

Mayoni is a member of The Fold and responsible for bringing Farah into the group.

She's beautiful, Asian and has brown hair. Also a former patient at Crescent Falls Mental Institution.

Carlton

Carlton is a member of The Fold and Mayoni's boyfriend. Carlton has been shaking people for years. The tip of his nose was shot off and he's a former patient at Crescent Falls Mental Institution.

Zashay

Zashay has Munchausen syndrome. Was dating Bones and is a former patient at Crescent Falls Mental Institution.

Nicola

Nicola is a former patient at Crescent Falls Mental Institution.

Denny

Denny is a former patient at Crescent Falls Mental Institution.

Eve

Eve is a former patient at Crescent Falls Mental Institution.

Phoenix

Phoenix is a former patient at Crescent Falls Mental Institution.

Wesley

Wesley is a former patient at Crescent Falls Mental Institution.

Gregory

Gregory is a former patient at Crescent Falls Mental Institution.

Swanson

Swanson is a former patient at Crescent Falls Mental Institution.

Vivica

Vivica is a former patient at Crescent Falls Mental Institution.

Lootz

Lootz is a former patient at Crescent Falls Mental Institution.

Dr. Weil

Dr. Weil is the leader of The Fold. Ten years back he was in charge of Crescent Falls, a mental institution, whose patients were tortured and castrated because they complained about the conditions of this facility. Dr. Weil tried to hold meetings with family members to advise of the conditions but nothing changed. So on Christmas Eve Dr. Weil released 15 patients who were in for treatable illnesses or sexual deviances. He injected the others with anesthesia and set Crescent Falls on fire. The remaining members make up The Fold.

OTHER CHARACTERS

Theo Cunningham

Theo was kicked in penis by Farah and her siblings as a child. His mother Dinette was killed by Mia and Shadow. He later killed Brownie and Chloe. He also showed Slade proof that she killed his brother Knox.

Sheriff Kramer

Sheriff Kramer deputized the Baker Boys to help remove a motorcycle club called the *Killer Bees* out of town. Things were great until an official police killed another officer while trying to take down the last member. Instead of admitting guilt, Sheriff Kramer turned on the Baker Boys and lied, saying they were responsible. But Knox secretly recorded the initial meeting on his cell phone from where he solicited their help.

Tornado

Tornado was murdered by Slade in the hallway of Platinum Lofts. He was arrested for Tornado's death.

Willie

Willie is Randy's father who was angry that he took over his drug business while he was in prison and wasn't willing to turn it back over upon his release. He later orchestrated his own son's murder.

GUEST STAR

Rasim Nami

Character from the book, "Prison Throne"

UP NEXT...

THE FOLD

BY T. STYLES

**A SURPRISE BOOK RELEASE.
COMING VERY, VERY, SOON**

**JOIN OUR EMAIL LIST BY TEXTING THE
WORD: CARTELBOOKS TO 22828 FOR
RELEASE INFO.**

The Cartel Publications Order Form
www.thecartelpublications.com
Inmates **ONLY** receive novels for $10.00 per book.
(Mail Order **MUST** come from inmate directly to receive discount)

Shyt List 1	_____	$15.00
Shyt List 2	_____	$15.00
Shyt List 3	_____	$15.00
Shyt List 4	_____	$15.00
Shyt List 5	_____	$15.00
Pitbulls In A Skirt	_____	$15.00
Pitbulls In A Skirt 2	_____	$15.00
Pitbulls In A Skirt 3	_____	$15.00
Pitbulls In A Skirt 4	_____	$15.00
Victoria's Secret	_____	$15.00
Poison 1	_____	$15.00
Poison 2	_____	$15.00
Hell Razor Honeys	_____	$15.00
Hell Razor Honeys 2	_____	$15.00
A Hustler's Son	_____	$15.00
A Hustler's Son 2	_____	$15.00
Black and Ugly	_____	$15.00
Black and Ugly As Ever	_____	$15.00
Year Of The Crackmom	_____	$15.00
Deadheads	_____	$15.00
The Face That Launched A	_____	$15.00
Thousand Bullets		
The Unusual Suspects	_____	$15.00
Miss Wayne & The Queens of DC	_____	$15.00
Paid In Blood (eBook Only)	_____	$15.00
Raunchy	_____	$15.00
Raunchy 2	_____	$15.00
Raunchy 3	_____	$15.00
Mad Maxxx	_____	$15.00
Quita's Dayscare Center	_____	$15.00
Quita's Dayscare Center 2	_____	$15.00
Pretty Kings	_____	$15.00
Pretty Kings 2	_____	$15.00
Pretty Kings 3	_____	$15.00
Silence Of The Nine	_____	$15.00
Silence Of The Nine 2	_____	$15.00
Prison Throne	_____	$15.00
Drunk & Hot Girls	_____	$15.00
Hersband Material	_____	$15.00
The End: How To Write A	_____	$15.00

By T. STYLES

Bestselling Novel In 30 Days (Non-Fiction Guide)

Upscale Kittens	_____	$15.00
Wake & Bake Boys	_____	$15.00
Young & Dumb	_____	$15.00
Young & Dumb 2:	_____	$15.00
Tranny 911	_____	$15.00
Tranny 911: Dixie's Rise	_____	$15.00
First Comes Love, Then Comes Murder	_____	$15.00
Luxury Tax	_____	$15.00
The Lying King	_____	$15.00
Crazy Kind Of Love	_____	$15.00
And They Call Me God	_____	$15.00
The Ungrateful Bastards	_____	$15.00
Lipstick Dom	_____	$15.00
A School of Dolls	_____	$15.00
Hoetic Justice	_____	$15.00
KALI: Raunchy Relived	_____	$15.00
Skeezers	_____	$15.00
You Kissed Me, Now I Own You	_____	$15.00
Nefarious	_____	$15.00
Redbone 3: The Rise of The Fold	_____	$15.00

(**Redbone 1 & 2** are **NOT** Cartel Publications novels and if ordered must be at **FULL** price of $15.00 each. No Exceptions.)

Please add $5.00 **PER BOOK** for shipping and handling.

The Cartel Publications * P.O. BOX 486 OWINGS MILLS MD 21117

Name: _____

Address: _____

City/State: _____

Contact/Email: _____

Please allow 5-7 BUSINESS days before shipping.

The Cartel Publications is NOT responsible for prison orders rejected.

NO PERSONAL CHECKS ACCEPTED

STAMPS NO LONGER ACCEPTED

322   REDBONE 3: THE RISE OF THE FOLD

CPSIA information can be obtained
at www.ICGtesting.com
Printed in the USA
LVOW08s1821021216
515532LV00001B/79/P